ESCAPE TO THE WEST
BOOK SIX

MORE THAN GOLD

NERYS LEIGH

PROLOGUE

April, 1870.

"She simply can't stay here. I won't have it."

"But darling..."

"She's twenty-nine, Albert. Twenty-nine! You've coddled her for too long and now she's a spinster old maid and it's your fault. You should have made her get married years ago. You aren't helping her, allowing her to stay here like this. It's not right."

"But darling..."

"I feel like this isn't even my home. I'm your wife. I should be the one managing the staff and running the household, but I'm not. She's always here, making decisions that aren't hers to make. I'm a stranger in my own home!"

"But darling..."

"The staff barely acknowledge that I'm the lady of the house."

"But darling..."

And there were the fake tears, right on cue.

Grace pursed her lips in disgust as she listened to her new stepmother yet again manipulate her ineffectual father. It was all she could do to not march into the parlor and give

1

them both a piece of her mind.

"Don't cry, darling. I understand this is hard for you."

"I don't think you do," Felicia sobbed. "I want to be your wife as a woman should be, but Grace won't let me. She won't let me do anything."

Grace's nails dug into her palms. She would have happily let her stepmother take over some of the duties in the house, but every time she suggested something, Felicia was always 'too busy', meaning getting some ridiculous beauty treatment, cackling with her insufferable friends, or spending Grace's father's money. The only reason she wanted Grace out of the house was so she could redecorate in her own garish taste and have no one there to rein in her spending.

"I can't force my daughter to leave. She has nowhere to go."

Felicia gave a watery sniff. "Of course you can't, but it isn't too late. You can arrange a marriage for her. Why, Mr. Howard has been widowed for more than six months. I'm sure he'd appreciate the chance to wed a slightly younger woman, even one of Grace's... appearance."

Slightly younger? Edward Howard was thirty years Grace's senior but could have passed for even more than that. He had hair growing out of his nose and both ears.

"And he's quite wealthy," Felicia went on. "I checked."

Of course the scheming harpy had checked. She'd been trying to get Grace out of the house for three months, ever since she'd beguiled her father into marriage.

Grace's father sighed. "Maybe you're right. It is time Grace married."

Grace gasped, her hand flying to her mouth. Surely he

didn't mean to force her into a loveless marriage with a man practically old enough to be her grandfather?

"I'll go and talk to Mr. Howard tomorrow. At least he lives nearby so I'll get to see her often. I should miss her if she wasn't here."

Felicia's voice turned to honey. "Of course you would, Sugarlump. You're a wonderful father. And this is the best thing for her, you'll see. I do love you."

"And I love you, my darling."

At the sound of Felicia's giggle, Grace backed away from the closed door, not wanting to hear any more.

She squeezed her eyes shut against stinging tears. He couldn't do this to her. She was his only child, he couldn't just cast her aside as if she meant nothing.

Pressing a hand to her mouth, she ran across the hall and up the wide staircase, not stopping until she was inside the sanctuary of her bedroom with the door securely locked. Throwing herself onto the bed, she buried her face into the pillow to muffle her sobs.

It wasn't like this was her fault. She wanted to fall in love and get married and have children, just like any woman did. She'd held onto hope even as every one of her thinner, prettier friends had found husbands, always believing that God had one special man for her. But as the years passed and the only men who ever showed any desire to court her were clearly more interested in her father's money than her, she'd begun to wonder if it was God's will that she get married at all.

What she did know, however, was that it wasn't His will that she marry an old man.

3

Wiping angrily at her eyes, she sat up. They wanted her gone? Fine, she'd go. But she would do it on her terms.

And those terms would not involve hairy ears.

~ ~ ~

"Is this all you have?"

Mrs. Wright looked up from her desk on the other side of the room, if you could call six feet away the other side of anything. "I'm afraid so. We only have two hundred and eighteen men looking for wives on our books at the moment. Are you certain not even one of them is suitable?"

Grace looked at the piles of papers on the table in front of her. She'd been in the tiny office of the Western Sunset Marriage Service for close to three hours, scrutinizing advertisement after advertisement from men in the west looking for wives. Somehow, there seemed to be something wrong with every single one of them. But she wasn't going to find perfection, she knew that. Why couldn't she decide on even one?

Was this why she was faced with being cast out of her own home by her father? Was she too fussy? Or was she simply too afraid to choose one, because then it would all be real? She'd be committing herself to leaving the only home she'd ever known. Traveling all the way across the country to a place she had no idea about, in order to marry a man she didn't know.

She'd be all alone.

Tears brimmed in her eyes and she turned away from Mrs. Wright, embarrassed and fumbling to open her reticule for a handkerchief. She heard a chair move on the wooden floor and a few moments later a hand rested on her shoulder.

"I can see your decision to travel across the country to marry isn't an easy one. Is there anything I can do to help?"

Grace dabbed at her eyes and looked up into Mrs. Wright's kind face. Seeing the older woman's compassion made her think of her mother. Even though it had been seven years since her passing, times like these made Grace miss her like it had only been yesterday.

She gave Mrs. Wright a small smile and looked down at the advertisements. "Thank you, but no. I really have no choice. It's this or hairy ears."

There were a few seconds of silence.

"Um... hairy ears?"

Grace raised her eyes to Mrs. Wright's now bemused face and burst into laughter. She might have been becoming a little hysterical.

"I'm so sorry," she gasped between giggles, "I'm feeling a little out of sorts today."

Mrs. Wright sat beside her, smiling kindly. "I understand. Not about hairy ears, but I understand. For many women who come here, this is their last resort."

Last resort. Was it truly Grace's last resort? She went through her options once again.

1) Marry Mr. Howard and his hairy ears.

2) Refuse to leave her home and spend the rest of her days arguing with her stepmother, at least until she bankrupted Grace's father. Or worse, get pushed out anyway.

3) Beg her spinster aunt to take her in and spend the rest of her days living under her ridiculously strict and hopelessly

5

outdated rules about behavior and dress.

4) Travel across the country to marry a man she'd never met and trust God to guide her to the right person.

There was a certain irony to the fact that the final option, the one she'd been forced into, was the only one that gave her any hope of maintaining some control over her own destiny. At least she got to choose the man she would be spending the rest of her life with.

"Last resort just about covers it," she said, her eyes drifting over the advertisements scattered across the table.

"Well then," Mrs. Wright said, clapping her hands together, "let's find you the perfect husband."

They sifted through the papers again, sorting them into piles of definitely no and possibly yes. The 'no' pile grew far faster than the 'yes'.

"This one seems interesting," Grace said, reading the advertisement from the young widower farmer again. She'd discounted him at first because he had two children and she had not the first idea how to take care of children, but considering she'd likely have her own one day, she'd need to learn at some point.

Mrs. Wright took the piece of paper from her. "Oh no, I'm so sorry, he's already asked a young lady to marry him and she said yes, just yesterday. This one should have been moved to the matched file."

Grace watched her place the advertisement to one side on the desk. Sighing, she turned back to the remaining two hundred and seventeen sheets of paper.

Her eyes settled on a name - Gabriel Silversmith. Ah yes, the gold mine owner. For some reason, that made her smile.

Mr. Silversmith owned a *gold* mine.

She picked up the advertisement. "What about this one? Is he still looking for a bride?"

"He certainly is. Would you like to try corresponding with him?"

Grace read the details again.

Age: 34

Location: Green Hill Creek, California.

Children: None.

Marital status: Never married.

Means: Owner of a profitable gold placer claim.

Requirements: A wife with whom to share life's ups and downs, challenges and victories. My deepest desire is to build a happy life together based on mutual support, respect and companionship.

It was almost poetic.

She nodded. "I think I would."

~ ~ ~

It was lunchtime by the time Grace returned home.

Her father and Felicia were already seated in the dining room while Mabel served them. Grace left her coat in the hallway and joined them at the table, her heart pattering in her chest.

They were halfway through the meal when her father cleared his throat, the usual indication he was about to say something he was uncomfortable with.

"Grace, I paid Mr. Howard a visit today."

"Did you?"

She knew he had. She'd followed him, to make sure he was going where she suspected he was. A deep sadness had settled over her as she watched him walk through the front gate of Mr. Howard's town house. Part of her had held onto a vain hope that he wouldn't betray her.

He cleared his throat again, glancing at Felicia who gave him the smallest of nods. "We had a very productive conversation."

"Did you?" she repeated, the pattering of her heart graduating to pounding.

"Um, yes. It seems that, that is to say, I suggested that perhaps he, um, I mean you and he, could, uh, enter into an arrangement."

Grace took another bite of her potatoes, although she'd lost her appetite. "What kind of arrangement?"

Her father swallowed and looked at Felicia again. "Um..."

Felicia rolled her eyes. "Just tell her." When he hesitated, she huffed out a breath and said to Grace, "Your father and I feel it would be beneficial if you had your own life in your own home. To that end, your father suggested to Mr. Howard that you and he should wed, and he was agreeable to the idea. You are to be married at the earliest opportunity."

Grace was gripping her knife and fork so tightly they dug into her palms. She placed them onto her plate and closed her eyes for a moment, praying for the strength to not break down in tears.

When she opened them again, she looked them both in

8

the eye. "I'm so grateful that you have seen fit to take all choice in my life away from me, since clearly I cannot be trusted to make my own decisions. However, I will not be able to marry Mr. Howard in whom, as you well know, I have no interest at all." When Felicia opened her mouth to speak, Grace raised her voice to drown her out. "Don't worry, Felicia, I won't be staying here any longer than I have to, so you'll be able to spend however much of my father's money as you wish."

Felicia raised a hand to her chest in feigned shock. "I don't know..."

"In fact," Grace went on, "neither of you will be forced to endure my presence at all in a few weeks, since I will be moving to California. But if that's not far enough away, please do say so and I will endeavor to leave the country entirely." She pushed back from the table and stood. "Now if you'll excuse me, I think I'll retire to my bedroom where I won't be in your way."

Ignoring her father's calls and Felicia's orders to him to "let her go", she strode from the room.

She only allowed the tears to come when she was safely in her bedroom.

CHAPTER 1

"If you do that for much longer you're going to need to stop in at the store to buy a new one."

Gabriel looked down at his hat and untwisted the brim, loosening his grip. "I may be a mite nervous."

Mrs. Jones gave him a sympathetic smile. "I'd be worried if you weren't. It would mean you didn't care if your new bride liked you or not."

Is that what it would mean? Right now he'd take it over feeling like his insides were scrabbling to get out.

Pastor Jones pointed along the railroad track at a plume of steam rising above the distant trees. "Here it comes."

Gabriel's gut dropped to his feet.

He hadn't been nearly this nervous the first time around. Then again, he hadn't considered how it could all go so horribly wrong.

He glanced at Mrs. Jones standing beside him. He wasn't one for talking about his feelings, but since his confidence seemed to be taking a nap, he needed the reassurance.

"Do you think it was my fault, what happened with Jo? Mrs. Parsons, I mean."

"Do you?" she said, not unkindly.

He'd considered that very question repeatedly. "I know I

10

got some things wrong. Badly wrong."

"You were in a difficult situation. To be honest, it's my belief that God never meant you and Jo to be together. Although He did use you to bring her here so she could meet Zach. I know it's not much comfort to you at this moment, but I also believe He will honor your part in that by bringing you the perfect wife. Just have faith that He knows what He's doing and it will all work out."

He gave her a non-committal nod and returned his attention to the approaching train. Faith wasn't something he'd ever had a great deal of, if any. But he appreciated what Pastor Jones and his wife were doing in helping him to get another bride after what happened the first time, so he wouldn't question her on it.

The train slowed to a halt in front of them, the breeze blowing a cloud of sooty steam across the station. Gabriel's grip tightened around the brim of his hat again.

Mrs. Jones patted his arm. "Don't worry. It's going to be all right."

She was too observant by half.

He swallowed and nodded and didn't say anything, in case it came out as shaky as he felt.

Passengers poured out of the train as the steam cleared, taking advantage of the stop to stretch their legs for a few minutes before it started off again. Gabriel moved his eyes from carriage to carriage, attempting to catch a glimpse of his new bride.

Unlike Jo, who had traveled with four other mail order brides, Grace was on her own. He'd worried a little about that. It took a week for the train to come all the way from

11

New York, a long time for a woman to be on her own without the protection of a man, although she hadn't seemed concerned in her letters.

He liked that about her. She was straightforward and practical. She'd adapt well to his life, he was sure of it. Almost sure.

This time, he'd made the right choice.

Probably.

Pastor Jones moved forward and Gabriel searched the crowd in that direction. And then he saw her.

Blonde hair gathered at her nape cascaded forward over one shoulder. Ruby red lips turned up in a smile while sparkling blue eyes peeked from beneath her bonnet. A rose pink dress fitted her slender curves, moving gracefully with her as she walked. The woman was stunning.

She sashayed up to Pastor Jones and walked past into the arms of a man waiting beyond him.

Gabriel's shoulders slumped. It wasn't her.

Distracted by the beautiful blonde, he hadn't noticed what the pastor was doing. He dragged his attention from the vision in pink to where he stood talking with someone Gabriel couldn't see.

His hat suffered more squashing as he waited for his first glimpse of his new bride. He hoped she wasn't ugly. He was a practical man and, on a basic level, one woman was as good as another. But still, since he would be looking at this one for the rest of his life, he'd prefer her to be pretty.

Then the pastor moved aside, and there she was.

Gabriel's eyes drifted down her form and back up. Grace Myers was a sturdy woman, walnut-brown hair, not overly tall, wearing a plain green skirt and blouse with a brown jacket. She wasn't slender like the blonde, but his tastes had always leaned toward more full-figured women anyway so that wasn't a bad thing. She wore an unadorned hat that matched her jacket and she had a fairly pleasant, if not beautiful, face. All in all, he could have done much worse.

He nodded approvingly. Not bad. Not bad at all.

Her eyes found his as she approached with the pastor, and Gabriel smiled. Her pink, full lips turned up uncertainly. They were nice lips.

"Miss Myers," Pastor Jones said, "may I introduce Gabriel Silversmith?"

"Mr. Silversmith, it's a pleasure to meet you."

Her tone was mellow and refined. A city voice. He suddenly felt very much like the country boy he was.

She offered him her hand and he quickly passed his crumpled hat into his left so he could take it, only then noticing how sweaty his palms had become. It was just as well she was wearing gloves.

"It's a real pleasure to meet you too, Miss Myers."

She nodded and pulled her hand away, clutching onto her reticule as hard as he was clutching onto his hat. A few seconds of awkward silence followed during which he racked his brain for something not stupid to say.

"And this is my wife," Pastor Jones finally said, to Gabriel's relief.

Mrs. Jones extended her hand. "We're so pleased to welcome you to our town, Miss Myers. I hope you'll be very happy here. Shall we go and fetch your luggage?"

Mrs. Jones continued to chat to Grace as they made their

13

way to the baggage car at the end of the train. Gabriel was grateful for it. If he'd known how nervous he was going to be, he'd have been more prepared with something to say. He hadn't been this way the first time around.

Three wooden trunks were being unloaded from the train. They looked expensive, overlaid with dark green leather and studded with brass. He jogged to his buckboard where he'd left it on the street and led Fred and Jed over to the small pile of luggage.

"Let me give you a hand with these," Pastor Jones said, wrapping his hand around the handle at one end of the nearest trunk.

Gabriel took the other and they lifted the heavy box into the buckboard. As they fetched the second one, he glanced at Grace. She was still talking quietly to Mrs. Jones, although her attention was on him. She looked away quickly when their eyes met.

"You all right?" Pastor Jones said quietly as they lifted the second trunk from the ground.

Gabriel nodded a little too quickly. "Yeah. I'm… yeah."

"It'll work out this time."

He wanted to ask how the pastor knew that, but he didn't want to risk Grace overhearing so he simply nodded again. The longer he could keep his first attempt at marriage from her, the better. He knew she'd find out eventually, but he hoped she'd be good and settled as his wife before that happened.

As they loaded the final trunk, he wondered where everything would go in his small, one roomed house. He'd probably need to get more furniture. He wasn't sure how to feel about that. He'd owned the place for two years and hadn't changed anything in the entire time. He was used to it. It was comfortable.

He almost rolled his eyes at himself. He sounded like an old man. He couldn't be set in his ways yet. He was only thirty-four. He didn't plan on being set in his ways for at least another ten years. He didn't want to be set in his ways until he was happy.

He slid the trunk into position behind the other two and again glanced back at Grace. Whether or not a wife would make him happy, he didn't know. The first one hadn't exactly fulfilled any of the needs he'd expected a wife to, but even then it had been nice having someone else around. Until that final day, at least.

But this time would be different. This time, he'd get things right from the start, make sure she knew what he expected of her.

This time, it would be a real marriage.

They walked the short distance to the church, Mrs. Jones and Grace in front and Pastor Jones walking with Gabriel who was leading Fred and Jed with the buckboard.

"Don't take this the wrong way," the pastor said in a low voice, "but I trust there won't be a repeat of what happened last time. I'd prefer not to have another of your wives turn up at the hotel in the middle of the night, no matter what the provocation."

Gabriel glanced at Grace ahead of them to make sure she couldn't hear. "I handled that badly, I know. It won't happen again."

The pastor stared at him long enough to make Gabriel

15

feel guilty, even though he meant what he said.

"Good," he said eventually, "I'm glad to hear it."

Gabriel nodded and wished they could walk faster.

When they arrived at the church, he set the brake on the buckboard and followed Grace and Mrs. Jones inside. He wasn't a regular at church, but this one was pleasant, as far as churches went, with its cream colored walls, high arched windows and polished wooden floors. It was as good a place as any to get wed.

Grace had stopped a little way along the aisle and his eyes drifted down his soon-to-be wife's body. She had a good figure, pleasantly rounded. He appreciated a woman who could fill his arms.

"Gabriel?"

He snapped his gaze up, startled. Had he been caught staring?

Pastor Jones edged past him in the aisle. "Would you and Miss Myers join me at the front?"

He swallowed and nodded, making a mental note to keep his eyes above the neck, at least until he and Grace were alone.

Pastor Jones and his wife headed to the platform at the front of the church and Gabriel was about to follow when an idea came to him.

Walking up to Grace, he held out his elbow. "Would you do me the honor of becoming my wife?"

Oh, that was good. He hadn't even thought of that in advance, it just came out. He smiled, just a little bit proud of himself. He could do this romance thing, no problem.

She stared at his arm as if it might bite her, not the

16

response he was expecting to his eloquent proposal. But then she gave him a small smile and slipped her arm slowly through his. Pleased he'd managed that much, he led her along the aisle to the front of the church and onto the platform.

The memory of his first wedding, on that very spot, flashed into his mind. He'd been sure things would work out back then. In fact, he hadn't even considered the possibility that they wouldn't.

He shook the thought away. Like Mrs. Jones said, he and Jo weren't meant for each other. But second time lucky, as they said.

Or was it third?

Pastor Jones smiled at both of them. "I've performed many marriages since my wife and I started working with the Western Sunset Marriage Service to match women in the east with the men in need of wives here, but it still makes me happy to see two people God has brought together promise their lives to each other."

Please don't mention the first time, Gabriel silently begged. Maybe he should have said something before Grace arrived, but he didn't want the pastor to think he was lying to his future wife.

"Grace, Gabriel," Pastor Jones continued, "marriage is a sacred vow before God and a pledge to each other to stand together, as one, for the rest of your lives. Whatever may come, you will never face it alone. It won't always be easy, but if you love and hold on to each other through it all, it will be right. Gabriel, do you have a ring? It's all right if you don't."

17

He glanced at Grace. "Uh, no, I don't."

Her shoulders lowered a little and for a moment he felt bad. It wasn't Grace's fault he'd picked the wrong woman in Jo.

Although just about the only thing that had gone right in that whole debacle had been that he'd never gone to the expense of buying her a ring. He wasn't giving Grace one either, not until he was good and sure she'd be sticking around.

"Well then," Pastor Jones went on, "Gabriel, would you repeat after me..."

"I, Gabriel Silversmith," he said after the pastor, "take you, Grace Margaret Myers, to be my wife, to have and to hold from this day forward, for better or for worse, for richer, for poorer, in sickness and in health, to love and to cherish; and I promise to be faithful to you until death parts us."

He held his breath as Grace said her vows, part of him expecting her to suddenly change her mind. He was probably just imagining her slight pause before promising to obey him.

He finally breathed out when the pastor said, "I now pronounce you man and wife. Congratulations, Mr. and Mrs. Silversmith. May God bless your marriage with much love, happiness and joy."

Gabriel turned to his new wife, just in case she wanted to kiss him, but all she did was give him a small smile that didn't reach her eyes. It didn't matter. There would be plenty of time for kissing, and more, later.

Mrs. Jones congratulated them both and then took Grace aside, speaking to her quietly.

Pastor Jones placed his hand on Gabriel's shoulder. "I'm

sure it will be different this time. Just... be patient with her. A little understanding goes a long way."

Gabriel frowned. What did that mean? He'd been patient with Jo and it had got him nowhere. "I won't mistreat her, if that's what you're thinking."

The pastor shook his head quickly and lowered his voice. "No, that's not what I'm suggesting at all. If I thought you were a man who would mistreat his wife, I wouldn't have helped you find one. I'm just saying, she seems nervous. You'll just need to give her time to get used to you and her new life. It's a big change for her."

Gabriel looked over at Grace where she was talking with Mrs. Jones on the other side of the church. "I will."

Things would be different this time. They had to be.

He wasn't doing it all again a third time.

CHAPTER 2

He didn't have ear hair, at least Grace could say that for him.

She looked up at her new husband as they stepped from the church back out into the cloudy day. He was taller than her, but she wasn't that tall to begin with. Dark, almost black hair that could probably do with a trim. A beard that could definitely use a trim, if not complete removal. Brown eyes, sun-darkened skin, lean body. Rugged, that was the word.

He wasn't handsome in an obvious way, not like some of the men she'd met in New York who had made her think, if only she were prettier, thinner. The men who had fawned over her friends but never her. Although her mother had always said it was her attitude that put them off, not her looks. She refused to simper and swoon, no matter how handsome the man.

But she'd never quite been able to embrace her mother's words. Good mothers always thought their daughters beautiful, no matter the reality. She'd held a fear, deep inside, that Gabriel would take one look at her and send her back on the next train, but he hadn't. At least there was that.

Mrs. Jones took her hands and smiled. "My husband and I live just down the street, so if you need anything at all, you come to us, day or night."

20

The pastor's wife was a compassionate soul. Grace almost wished she could stay with her. "I will, thank you. You've been very kind."

Glancing at Gabriel who had wandered off to his buckboard, Mrs. Jones leaned in close and lowered her voice. "He's a bit rough around the edges, but be patient. Underneath it all, he's got it in him to be a good man."

Grace wasn't sure what to make of that, so she simply replied, "Thank you. I'll do my best."

She followed Gabriel to the buckboard and waited. He ignored her, walked around to the other side, and climbed up to the driver's seat.

When she didn't move, he looked down at her. "Aren't you getting in?"

She was so shocked that for a few moments she didn't know what to say. Annoyance rapidly replaced her astonishment at his lack of manners.

"Aren't you going to help me up?"

"Why? Something wrong with your legs?" His gaze went to her skirt.

She opened her mouth and closed it again. She'd have thought he was being facetious, if he hadn't looked so completely serious. Rough around the edges indeed. Sighing, she gathered her skirts and climbed up beside him. *Patience*, she reminded herself, glancing over at Mrs. Jones where she stood beside the pastor at the church door.

Mrs. Jones gave her a small shrug and a sympathetic smile, and waved. Grace waved back as they pulled away, feeling a little bereft at leaving the woman who'd been so kind to her, and more than a little nervous at the prospect of being alone with the man she'd just married.

They reached the end of the road and turned right onto a busier thoroughfare. There were more people here than she'd seen in the town so far, and shop fronts lined the street. They passed a post office and Grace reminded herself to write to her father when she reached her new home to let him know she'd arrived safely. As if he cared.

"I have to make a stop first, but then we'll head home," Gabriel said, guiding the buckboard left into a side road. Fifty yards or so later he brought them to a halt and set the brake. "I'll be right back."

She watched him jog up a path lined with fruit bushes to the front door of a small house and knock. There were four trees crammed into the modest sized garden, two apples and two oranges. The owners clearly loved their fruit.

A tall thin man opened the door. Gabriel spoke to him and he was replaced by a short round woman who handed him a serving dish covered with a red checked cloth. As Gabriel walked back to the road, the woman waved to Grace with a warm smile. Grace waved back. The residents of the town seemed friendly enough.

Gabriel lodged the covered serving dish amongst her luggage and climbed back up beside her. The most incredible aroma rose to caress her nasal passages.

"What's in the dish?" she said, twisting around to get a better nose-full of the delicious smell.

He clicked his tongue to the horses and they started off again. "Beef stew. Best you'll ever taste."

She glanced back at the house. "Who were those people?"

"Mr. and Mrs. Goodwin. Mrs. Goodwin is the best cook this side of, well, anywhere. She likes to welcome new people to the town with her stew. She told me to stop by before we left."

"It smells delicious." She took another deep breath of the wonderful aroma.

"Tastes even better, believe me."

The houses either side of the road they followed stretched farther and farther apart and soon petered out altogether as they left the town behind them. Green Hill Creek could hardly be classed as a metropolis. From what Grace had seen, it barely qualified as a town. Still, she liked the countryside so that wasn't necessarily a bad thing. When she was younger she'd often accompanied her parents on trips out of the city, and she always enjoyed the feeling of space and freedom from the dirty, crowded New York streets.

She looked out over the cultivated fields they drove through to the mountains beyond and drew in a deep breath of clean, fresh air. Yes, she could definitely get used to this.

"How far is your house?" she asked, watching a shimmering blue butterfly flit past.

"'Bout an hour or so out of town, depending on how fast you go."

She whipped her head around to gape at him. "An *hour*?"

He nodded, seemingly oblivious to her shock.

She tried to remember if he'd mentioned the remoteness of his home in any of the letters she received from him but came up empty. There hadn't been many of them, and his were never very long or detailed. Surely she would have noticed if he'd said he lived a whole hour from civilization.

"Are there other houses around yours?" Maybe he lived in a hamlet, away from the town but close to other people.

"Nope, nothing out there except for my place. It's up in the foothills, too rocky for farming or ranching. Most of the folks round here are either farmers or ranchers or work in the town. There are the men who work in the mines, but a lot of those have closed down, now it's getting harder to find the gold."

She looked at the mountains again. They had seemed pretty, but now they appeared barren and remote. "Will we be coming into town much?"

"You can go in whenever you like. I've got a buggy you can use."

"On my own?"

He glanced at her. "Sure. Is that a problem?"

Back at home she'd rarely gone out alone. It just wasn't done.

But this was a long way from New York and she wasn't some simpering, helpless woman who couldn't take care of herself. "No, it's not a problem."

He nodded and looked forward again and she lapsed into silence. It wasn't a problem. She was a strong woman. She'd run her father's household for the past seven years, she could cope with whatever life threw at her. Fear was a perfectly normal response to a situation such as traveling clear across the country to marry a man she'd never met and then being faced with the prospect of living miles from anyone else. It was no problem at all.

As the horses continued to plod in the direction of her

24

new home and Gabriel failed to offer up anything more in the way of explanation as to his living situation, she began listing in her mind the good things about being there, on the way to her new home in the middle of nowhere, miles from anyone else.

1) The scenery was stunning.

2) Gabriel wasn't hideously ugly.

3) The scenery was stunning.

4) The scenery...

She sighed quietly. This wasn't going to be easy.

~ ~ ~

"There it is," Gabriel announced.

Grace tore her attention from a shape in the distance that looked disturbingly like a bear but couldn't possibly have been because she couldn't cope with a bear on top of everything else. All she saw ahead of them was a group of derelict buildings.

"There what is?"

"Home sweet home."

She glanced at him to check if he was looking at the same thing she was. "You... you mean those buildings?"

He nodded. "I know they ain't much to look at, but they're warm and dry and..." He frowned, apparently trying to come up with something else nice to say about the shabby looking place. Then his face lit up. "Cozy!"

"Cozy," she murmured, regarding her new home with trepidation.

Maybe it was better on the inside.

She looked in the direction she'd seen the not-bear, but it was gone. The road they'd followed out of town had become a track through farmland, then two ruts worn into the earth as the terrain had turned to a gentle slope. She turned to look behind them but couldn't see the town any longer through the trees and rocky outcrops they'd passed. Somehow, losing that last sight of civilization made her feel very alone.

Gabriel brought the buckboard to a halt when they reached the buildings and set the brake. Grace looked around. To the left was what she assumed was the house, if you could use so generous a word. It was tiny, no more than fifteen feet long, with a door, two windows, a porch spanning the front, and not much else. Across the dusty yard, to her right, were two barns. Beyond the barns was a fenced field and a smaller enclosure where several chickens pecked at the earth. And that was it.

She looked around to check if she'd missed anything. She hadn't.

"You can go right on in," Gabriel said, nodding towards the house. "I'll bring your luggage in just now."

He jumped down from the buckboard and moved to unhitch the horses, once again making no move to assist her down. At least she wasn't surprised this time.

She climbed down to the packed earth yard and wandered towards the house, looking around her as she walked. Up close, the place wasn't as derelict as she'd at first thought. Yes, there were overgrown weeds just about everywhere, and some sort of large metal contraption she couldn't identify sat rusting between the barns, but the buildings themselves looked solid. At least, they didn't

26

appear in immediate danger of collapsing on her in her sleep.

It all just needed some work, she told herself. A few potted plants, some flowers, and it would be transformed into a beautiful home.

She almost believed it.

A deep *woof* brought her to a sudden halt. She spun round, images of a pack of vicious wolves racing to tear her to shreds flashing through her mind, and froze at the sight of the biggest dog she'd ever seen padding towards her from the direction of one of the barns.

"Be nice, Brute," Gabriel said, glancing towards it. "That there's Grace and she's going to be living with us from now on. I told you about her." He looked at Grace. "That's Brutus. Don't mind him, he won't hurt you."

She loved dogs. She'd had two of her own growing up. Those had both, however, been significantly smaller than the behemoth now approaching her. Brutus was a pale golden brown with a darker muzzle and ears and stood as tall as her thigh, with a solid, muscular body and an excess of skin drooping around his face. Huge as he was, he didn't appear in any way threatening, so she stood up straight, took a deep breath, and waited for him to reach her.

"Good afternoon, Brutus," she said, holding out her hand when he got closer. "It's a pleasure to meet you."

He stretched his head forward to sniff at her fingers, his tail slowly moving from side to side. Evidently deciding she was acceptable, he moved closer and sat down, looking up at her. She gently moved her hand to stroke his head and his tail swished faster across the ground. Encouraged, she rubbed both his ears. His tongue lolled from his mouth and he leaned

27

happily into her touch.

For the first time since she'd arrived, a genuine smile touched her lips. "I hope you and I are going to be great friends, Brutus."

Brutus. It didn't fit him. Certainly he looked intimidating, but he seemed about as threatening as a duckling.

Giving his ears a final scratch, she turned back to the house and walked up the steps to the porch. Behind her she heard Brutus shake his head then pad up the steps after her, his claws clicking on the wooden porch. When she opened the door, he waited for her to walk inside then followed her.

She looked around at her new home. It didn't take long. Somehow, the interior appeared even smaller than the outside. She wasn't entirely sure what she'd been expecting, but it wasn't this. Gabriel had told her in his letters that he owned a placer claim that produced a good amount of gold. If that was true, he wasn't putting his profits into where he lived.

The interior of the house was a single room. A kitchen area sat to her right, with a cupboard and hutch, a small stove, and a rustic wooden table surrounded by four mismatched chairs. In front of her were two somewhat threadbare upholstered chairs with a low table between them. Leaning against the wall was a tall bookcase housing various household items and haphazardly folded clothing, but no books. Against the wall to her left was a double bed with a washstand and chest of drawers beside it. Clothing hung from hooks on the wall in the corner by the bed.

And that was more or less it.

Brutus wandered over to the stove and flopped down on

a rug beside it.

Grace looked around again, feeling a little numb. Was this it? Was this her new life with her new husband? Was this what she'd moved all the way across the country for?

Well, no, she'd moved all the way across the country to find a place where she was wanted. But did Gabriel truly want her, or would any woman have done? Did she even want to be here?

Unbidden tears brimmed in her eyes and she wiped at them. "Is this where you want me, Lord?" she whispered.

How could this possibly be right? How could she be meant to be here?

A wet nose pushed into her palm and she looked down to see Brutus standing beside her. He whined, tentatively wagging his tail.

She sniffed and stroked his silky head. "At least you care how I feel."

At the sound of footsteps on the porch outside she blinked rapidly and wiped the rest of her tears away.

Gabriel walked in carrying one of her heavy trunks and placed it on the floor by the bed.

"I cleared you some space," he said, pointing to three empty hooks on the wall and an empty shelf on the bookcase. "And the middle two drawers are empty." He stood looking at the chest of drawers for a few seconds, his fingers tapping against his thigh. "I, um, I know this is probably smaller than what you're used to, but as I said, it's cozy and dry and... and..." He nodded. "Anyway, I'll bring the rest of your things in."

She watched him walk out again then turned to look at

the spaces he'd cleared for her. At home she'd had an entire chest of drawers and two matching armoires for her clothing. They were a set, designed especially for her sixteenth birthday, a gift from her parents. The cabinet maker had been French. Not that it mattered where he was from, but she'd been impressed when her father told her all the same.

She missed her home, and her room, and her father. She missed her life.

Shaking her head, she wiped at her eyes again. She'd only been here five minutes. All she needed was time to get used to her new home. It wasn't so bad. It appeared clean and there were pretty curtains at the windows and cushions on the chairs and the walls were painted a fresh white. It wasn't perfect, but she could work with it. It would be fine. It would all be fine.

She walked over to her trunk, Brutus padding after her.

It would all be just fine.

~ ~ ~

Gabriel brought her other two trunks in and left her to unpack.

By some careful folding and arranging, she managed to fit her everyday things into the drawers, shelf and hooks she'd been given. The rest of her clothing, her fancier outfits, she left in one of the trunks. There was nowhere to hang them and she wasn't sure when she'd need them anyway, so far from town as she was. She'd choose something to wear to church when Saturday came round and deal with what to do with it then.

She placed her most important possession, the photograph of her with her mother and father when she was twenty, on the table beside the bed. Sitting on the covers, she reached out to rub away a mark from the silver frame with her thumb.

"I know you'd tell me to try my best, Mama," she whispered, "so that's what I'm going to do. I know this isn't what you wanted for me, but I finally got a man to marry me."

She smiled as she said it, hoping the joke would make her feel better. It didn't.

Brutus raised his head from the rug where he lay, looking towards the door. A few seconds later, Gabriel walked in. He was carrying the serving dish he'd brought from the Goodwin's house. Brutus sniffed at the air.

Gabriel looked at the filled hooks on the wall and the no longer empty shelf on the bookcase as he placed the dish onto the table. "You find enough space to put everything?"

Brutus hauled himself to his feet and padded to the table. Gabriel moved the dish into the center, away from his questing nose.

Her first instinct was to say yes, purely out of politeness. But she reminded herself that this was her home now, and she had a right to see that her own needs were met too.

"I unpacked the things I'll need every day, but there are still some clothes there wasn't room for."

He glanced at the corner of the room where their clothing hung. "I reckon I could put more hooks up."

She would rather have had a wardrobe where her clothes would be protected from dust, but it would probably be better to bring that up at a later date, when they were both more accustomed to her being there. "Thank you, that would be very helpful."

He nodded and walked over to the stove. Brutus eyed the dish on the table, his tongue snaking out over his lips.

"I'll set Mrs. Goodwin's stew warming," Gabriel said, taking a box of matches from a drawer, "then we can eat soon. If you're hungry now, there's bread and such in the cupboard."

She hadn't eaten for some time, but nerves had dampened her appetite. "I'm all right, thank you."

Brutus glanced at Gabriel where he was crouched to light the firebox in the stove. Apparently reassured his master wasn't watching, he rested his chin on the table and inched his nose towards the serving dish.

"Well, whenever you want anything, just take it," Gabriel said, seemingly oblivious to his dog's designs on their supper. "There's a root cellar under the house. Entrance is round the side."

"Mm hmm." Covering her mouth to hide her smile, Grace nodded vaguely, mesmerized by Brutus' attempts to reach the food. She possibly should have said something, but she wanted to see what would happen.

"It's cool down there so I keep all the perishables there too." He stoked the flame he'd ignited, added some sticks, pushed the firebox closed and rose to his feet.

Brutus stretched his neck across the table, his front paws almost leaving the floor as he strained to reach the delicious smelling food. With his nose within a couple of inches of the dish, he reached out his tongue.

32

Gabriel walked to the table and picked up the dish just before it was licked. Brutus dropped back to the floor and looked up at him with a whine. Grace wasn't sure if it was guilt or accusation on his face.

Gabriel shook his head. "Anyone would think you never got fed, instead of eating me out of house and home."

Brutus wagged his tail and looked pointedly at the dish.

Gabriel turned away and leaned down to place it in the oven. Then he opened a cupboard, took out a carrot, and handed it to the dog.

"You can wait like the rest of us."

Brutus carried the carrot to his rug and settled down to eat.

Somehow, the brief exchange between man and dog served to reassure Grace a little. If her new husband cared about his dog, that meant he could care about her too. Didn't it?

Not that she was comparing herself to a dog.

"Would you like to rest some?" Gabriel said, drawing her attention from Brutus and his carrot. He pushed his hands into his pockets then pulled them out again. "Or I could show you around the place." He paused. "If you'd like."

"I'd like that." Maybe knowing more about her new home would make her feel better about it.

He nodded and glanced at Brutus as he headed for the door. "You coming?"

Brutus had the carrot lodged upright between his paws while he nibbled at the end. He flicked his eyes to Gabriel for a moment then lowered them back to the carrot. Gabriel shrugged one shoulder and walked out.

Grace followed him through the door, stifling a sigh. At least he'd left it open for her. But they were going to have to have a detailed discussion about manners at some point in the near future.

When she joined him outside, he was pulling a small leather pouch from his pocket. He unwound the thong holding it closed, took out a brown lump, and pushed it into his cheek. Grace scrunched her nose in disgust. Bad manners paled into insignificance when it came to chewing tobacco.

She opened her mouth to say something then closed it again, reminding herself she'd been there less than half an hour.

Get settled in first, start work on her husband's less desirable qualities later.

He nodded to a rough table that stood against the wall of the house beside a large barrel, speaking around the lump of tobacco in his mouth. "That's for washing the dishes. Water's in the barrel. I fill it up every morning from the stream. I'll show you where that is for when you need to do it."

Their water came from a stream? Was that even hygienic? "You don't have a pump?"

He trudged down the steps to the yard. "Never had no need for one. Stream's not far. It comes down off the mountain, so it's clean."

She wanted to ask if there was no dirt in the mountains but didn't. If he'd survived this long, she probably would, at least for now. She hoped.

She followed slowly down the steps, her gaze drawn to the vista to her right where the valley stretched into the distance. For much of the train journey she'd marveled at the wide open spaces they traveled through. She'd never imagined she'd have such a view right on her doorstep. It *almost* made up for the lack of plumbing.

Gabriel glanced back at her from where he stood at the doorway to one of the barns. "Something wrong?"

Not even aware she'd stopped, she resumed walking. "I was just admiring the view."

He looked at the sumptuous greens and browns of the wide valley, the gray-blue mountains in the distance, and the wide, cloud-shrouded sky. God's majestic creation laid out before them in all its glory.

"It's all right, I guess."

She had to stop herself from groaning out loud. Who was this man, who couldn't see such beauty right in front of him? She'd only just met him and she was already beginning to wonder if they'd ever see anything the same way. How would they ever get along?

"This barn's for all my tools and equipment and such."

She walked up beside him and peered around the dim interior.

"And the buggy's here, for whenever you want it."

She studied the slightly shabby one-horse buggy, with its seat just big enough to fit two people, if they were close. "Will you teach me how to hitch it to the horse?"

She'd never had to do that at home since there was always a servant to do it for her. She wished now she'd paid attention.

"Sure."

The second barn stood roughly ten feet from the first. As

they walked past the gap between the two, he spat a stream of tobacco-laced saliva into the scrubby grass. She recoiled in disgust and looked away.

Three stalls took up half of the space inside of the second barn and a strong smell of rat waste filled the enclosed space, making her shudder. She hated rats.

"This is where the horses and goat sleep." He pointed to a line of barrels against the back wall. "That's their feed. Make sure you close the lids good and tight after you've used them. Hay's up top." He pointed to a ladder leading to an opening in the ceiling.

She nodded, trying to breathe without actually breathing. He looked around, hands on his hips, as if trying to think of something else to say.

"I'll take care of the animals most of the time, but I'll show you what to do so you'll know for when I'm not here."

She nodded again. Could one be asphyxiated from holding one's breath?

"All right then," he said. "I suppose I'll show you the animals now."

She nodded a third time and rushed back outside, surreptitiously gulping in a few lungfuls of fresh air. If she was going to spend any time in that barn at all, something would need to be done about the smell.

Beside the barn was an enclosure with a wooden shack in the center. Eight chickens pecked in the grass surrounding it. Beyond the chickens was a large, fenced field where the horses who'd pulled the buckboard were grazing, along with a brown goat.

The goat trotted over to them where they stood at the

fence.

She reached through to rub its head. It tried to eat her sleeve. "What's his name?"

"Hasn't really got one. I just call it Goat. And it's a she. She's for milking, not eating, so don't go killing her or nothing."

No chance of that. "Understood."

"And be careful around her. If she can find a way out, she will. Always shut the gate."

"I will."

"The chickens are for laying, but if any of them stop, you can kill that one for eating."

She stared at him in horror. "I can *what*?"

"The chickens." He indicated the birds which carried on rummaging through the soil for food, blissfully oblivious to any mention of their demise. "If any of them can't lay anymore, we can eat it."

"You're expecting me to kill a chicken?" She'd never killed anything in her life. Not even a spider.

He looked confused. "You don't eat chicken in New York City?"

"Well, yes, but we don't kill them."

It was his turn to look horrified. "You eat them *alive*?"

"No! But we don't kill them. At least, I don't kill them. Of course *someone* kills them, but we just buy them from the butcher." She looked around, suddenly realizing that the nearest butcher was probably back in Green Hill Creek, an hour's ride away.

"Would you prefer me to kill them?" His mildly amused expression made her feel foolish.

37

"Yes. No!" She sighed, watching the chickens. "How can you kill something you've looked after?"

He pushed his hands into his pockets and shrugged. "Don't know. So far, I've never had to do it. Can't imagine it'll be a problem though. They're only chickens."

His callous attitude annoyed her.

"They're living things. They have feelings, in their own way. I know it's for eating, but killing something shouldn't be easy, even if it is only a chicken."

He stared at the chickens and a melancholy look passed across his face. "It shouldn't, but sometimes it has to be."

It was a strange thing to say. It almost sounded as if he was used to killing. That was something she should know about her new husband, wasn't it? Although she was now a little nervous about what the answer would be if she asked him about it.

She moved closer to where he stood by the fence, his arms resting on the top as he gazed across the grassy field. "What do you mean, sometimes killing has to be easy?"

He glanced at her from the corner of his eye. "You ask a lot of questions."

She hadn't asked him half of the questions she wanted to. "How else are we supposed to get to know one another?"

He shrugged and went back to staring across the field, evidently unwilling to supply any further information on what, or who, he'd killed.

She decided to change the subject. "What are the horses' names? And no, I'm not apologizing that that's another question."

To her surprise, a small smile flitted across his face.

38

"They're Jed and Fred."

She studied the two identical bay geldings. "Which one's which?"

He pointed to the one on the left. "Fred." And the one on the right. "Jed."

"How do you tell the difference?" She squinted at them, as if that would help.

He looked at her as if she was dense. "Jed's the lighter colored one. And they look completely different. Their faces aren't even the same."

"Oh." They looked exactly the same to her. Hopefully they knew their own names, if she ever had to call one of them.

He stepped back from the fence. "Food won't be ready yet so I reckon I can show you where to get the water now."

They walked up the slope from the house towards a wooded area. He led her along a well-trodden path through the trees, following the sound of running water. After less than a minute, they came to a wide stream winding around boulders and rocky outcrops and tumbling over a small waterfall. Birds twittered in the branches overhead and insects buzzed amongst tufts of grass and wildflowers.

Enchanted, Grace turned in a circle, taking it all in. "Oh, this is so pretty."

Gabriel pushed his hands into his pockets and smiled. "It is real nice here."

The smile transformed his face. Perhaps he was a little more attractive than she'd given him credit for.

Embarrassed that she might be caught staring, she looked away and wandered to the stream's edge, peering into the clear water. After a few seconds, he walked up beside her and stood silently, gazing into the trees across from them.

Try as she might, she couldn't stop thinking about what he'd said about killing. She had to know what he'd meant. "Have you killed many animals?"

He shrugged. "Haven't kept track. I grew up on a farm so I started young."

A farm, that made sense. But she couldn't shake the feeling there was more. "Have you killed any people?"

"Too many."

All the breath left her body. "I... what?"

He glanced at her. "I fought in the war."

Her lungs started working again. She didn't think she'd ever felt more relieved in her life. "Oh. Yes. Of course. I'm sorry."

He turned from the stream. "Well, I reckon the food'll be just about ready by now. We ought to get back."

Part of her wanted to ask him about the war, but the rest of her was afraid to. But they didn't know each other yet. Maybe once they did, he'd tell her.

By the time they returned to the house, the aroma of Mrs. Goodwin's warming stew had filled the room. Brutus, having finished his carrot, was lying facing the stove with his head on his paws and his eyes on the oven door. When they walked in his tail thumped against the floor and he flicked his nose between the oven and Gabriel. Grace couldn't blame him. The smell of the stew was making her stomach rumble.

Gabriel took a cloth from a hook, opened the oven door, and took the dish out, placing it on the top. Brutus stood and wagged his tail, eyes fixed on his every move.

"Looks like it's ready. Plates are in the hutch." He picked up the dish and carried it to the table.

She sighed quietly. Had she really been expecting him to serve her, just because it was their first meal together?

He took a bowl from the hutch, spooned in some of the stew, added some bread he cut from a loaf he took from a breadbox that sat on the cupboard, and carried it outside. Brutus rushed out after him.

All five of the plates in the hutch were made of tin, their surfaces scratched and dull from years of use. The kind of plates a miner might use, Grace imagined. Maybe they'd come with the house. The cutlery was in a drawer and she sorted through it until she found an unmarked knife and fork for herself. She didn't bother doing the same for Gabriel. She was going to have a lot of cleaning to do.

He had set the serving dish in the center of the table and she frowned at the lack of anything to protect the wooden surface from the heat. Not that it mattered much. The tabletop was covered with marks anyway. Maybe he had a tablecloth somewhere.

She glanced around her. Or maybe not.

He returned from the porch, pulled a chair back from the table, and dropped into it. "Fill the whole plate, darlin'."

Darlin'?

As a general rule, she had no objection to serving her husband his food. But his utter lack of even a little consideration for her after her long journey just to become his wife was going too far. She was tired, hungry, scared, and now she was angry. Enough was enough.

She placed one plate in front of each of them, picked up

41

the serving spoon he'd used to fill Brutus' bowl, and very deliberately filled her own plate. Then she sat down.

His eyes flicked to the empty plate in front of him. "Haven't you forgotten something?"

She picked up her knife and fork. "I don't think so. Oh, did you want to say the blessing before I eat?"

"No, I don't want to say the blessing! Where's my food?"

She donned her most cherubic smile and nodded at the serving dish. "Right there. Better hurry, wouldn't want it to get cold."

He opened his mouth and closed it again. Shaking his head, he picked up the spoon and mumbled something about being the husband as he loaded his plate with food.

CHAPTER 3

Gabriel was confused.

In his experience, which, admittedly, chiefly consisted of his own mother and father, the duties of a husband and wife were clearly defined. The husband did the work, providing for the family in whatever way he had. It was also acceptable for him to look after the horses and, at a stretch, any other animals they might have. In return, the wife did everything in the home, which included serving meals and cleaning up afterwards.

So why had he dished out his own food and, more importantly, why was he now standing beside Grace at the wash tub and drying the wet dishes she handed to him?

Maybe things were different in the east. That must be it. He'd need to teach his new wife how they did things in the west, the proper way. But as it was only her first day, he could help out for now.

He glanced at her out of the corner of his eye, his gaze drifting down. At least he knew there were certain things they did the same everywhere. He didn't mind drying a few dishes if it got them to the good parts of marriage faster.

While Grace paid a visit to the privy when they were done, he carried the dry dishes inside and put them away.

Then he sat at the table, smoothed his hair back, and waited. After a few seconds, he huffed a breath into his hand and sniffed. It smelled of tobacco. Nothing wrong with that.

When she walked through the door he sat up straight and gave her his best smile. Her lips turned up hesitantly, just for a moment.

They were a tempting shade of pink, her lips. Full and plump. He'd thought Jo pretty, if a mite on the skinny side, but Grace had the kind of curves that drew a man's attention and wouldn't let go. He'd have to watch the other men around her. He wouldn't have anyone looking at his wife the way he had been.

She walked past him to the cupboard and he followed her movements, allowing his gaze to roam down her back and over the pleasing mound of her rump. Oh yes, he was going to enjoy fulfilling his husbandly duties with her, no doubt about it.

And speaking of husbandly duties...

He rose and walked across the room to her, stopping just a foot away when she turned around.

"You're a real handsome woman, Grace," he said, sliding his hands around her waist and leaning in for their first kiss.

A fist slammed into the side of his face, whipping his head around and sending him reeling backwards.

She grabbed a skillet from the cupboard and held it in front of her like a weapon. "What are you *doing*?!"

He shook his head to clear it. The woman had a right hook most men would have been proud of. "What do you think I'm doing? We're married. We're going to do what

44

married folks do."

It was a perfectly natural assumption, as far as he was concerned.

But not for her, apparently. "We've known each other for less than three hours and you expect me to just allow you to have your way with me?"

What was going on here? "Uh... yes?"

She gasped in a horrified breath. "You... you... uncouth *brute!*"

He was fairly sure *uncouth* was a bad thing.

Drawing himself up, he pointed his finger at her. "Now wait just a minute. We're legally wed. It's not like you'll be whoring yourself out to me. I'm your husband."

Her eyes looked like they could pop right out of her head. "*Whoring?!*"

It may have been a poor choice of words.

He raised both hands, palms out in surrender. "That ain't what I meant. I'm just saying that it's natural for a husband and wife to want to..."

"Well I don't want to, so you keep your hands to yourself!" She brandished the pan, forcing him to step back.

He rubbed at his aching face. If she could do that with just her fist, no telling what kind of damage she could do with a skillet.

He decided to try reasoning with her, from a safe distance. "I know we haven't been together for long, but we'd been writing letters to each other for nigh on three months before you came. I reckon we know each other plenty. I promise I'll be real gentle and..."

"You won't be gentle. You won't be anything." She

45

waved the skillet. "Because it *isn't happening*!"

An idea came to him. Maybe she was simply so innocent and pure that she had no idea about what went on in the marriage bed. He didn't have much experience in dealing with women like that, but it shouldn't be too difficult to set her mind at ease. It was like taming a skittish horse. He just had to gain her trust.

"Grace, sweetheart," he said, softening his voice, "when a man and a woman get wed, there's certain things they do on their wedding night. They're not unpleasant things and you have nothing to be afraid of..."

"I'm twenty-nine years old, Mr. Silversmith, I know what intercourse is. And we aren't having any!"

Did she mean she wasn't as pure as he assumed? Surely he couldn't have married a second already pregnant woman. "Are you expecting?"

Her ire turned to confusion. "Expecting what?"

"A baby."

Her confusion shot back through ire and plunged straight into outrage. "Are you suggesting I have had relations out of wedlock? And that I look like I'm with *child*?!" She looked down at herself.

"No! I just... I don't..." He ran one hand over his hair. Women were impossible. It was all so much easier when he just paid them, did the deed, and left. "Look, we're husband and wife and that means you have certain duties. Now you must have known this would happen."

"Of course I knew we would... would... have relations. But not as soon as I arrived." She waved the skillet at him. "I am not just a... a... *body* you can have your way with whenever you please! I have a mind. And feelings."

Feelings. Why did women have to make everything about feelings?

"Well, what do you expect me to do?"

She stood up straight, lifting her chin. "I expect you to woo me."

"*Woo?*"

"Yes, woo."

"But I already asked you to marry me and paid for you to come here. What more do you want?"

"I want you to..." She looked at the window, as if that would provide the answer. "I want us to get to know each other, to talk and spend time together. Find out about each other, who we are, what we like and don't like. I want you to do nice things for me, like bring me flowers and... and... things like that." Her shoulders slumped, the skillet dropping to her side. "I want you to care about me."

Moisture glistened in her eyes and she lowered her gaze, her lips pressed into a line.

He stared at her in horror. "Are you crying?"

She shook her head. A tear caught the light as it plopped to the floor, leaving a tiny circle of wet on the wood.

He rubbed the back of his neck, trying not to panic. He hated it when women cried. His mother had cried sometimes. Those had been the worst moments of his childhood.

"Please don't cry." He took a step towards her, reaching out.

The skillet whipped up between them, forcing him back again. She watched him suspiciously, wiping at her eyes with her free hand.

47

He raised both palms towards her. "I'm not going to try anything, I swear."

"You'd better not."

Yet again, things were not going as he thought they would. Maybe he should have expected this after the first time. But the tears glistening on her cheeks were effectively dampening his ardor anyway. Perhaps he should try being nice to her, like she wanted. That couldn't hurt.

He stepped back, lowering his hands to his sides. "Are you tired? I reckon you must be, after your journey on the train."

She lowered the skillet slightly. "I am tired. I had hardly any sleep the entire time. It was so noisy and uncomfortable and everything was always moving."

That must be it! She was tired. With a good night's sleep in her she'd no doubt be far more amenable to his advances. He could wait. His gaze slid down. He didn't want to wait, but he could.

"Well, it's nice and quiet here," he said, waving one hand around. "And no moving."

She smiled a little. "That's true."

Now she was no longer crying, his natural inclinations were returning. He needed some fresh air.

"Look, I'm going to go and see to the animals. Why don't you wash up and... and... do whatever women do at night." He didn't know what that was, but he knew it involved more than simply stripping off clothing and getting into bed. The whole process was a mystery to him, both the what and the why. "Then you can get to bed early and have a good long sleep. You'll feel much better in the morning."

She eyed him uncertainly. "You aren't expecting us to..." She waggled the skillet at the bed.

"No, I swear I won't do anything. I can see you're not ready tonight and I understand that." His eyes drifted down. He couldn't help it. "I can't say I'm not disappointed. You are a real attractive woman. But I can wait."

To his astonishment, her cheeks colored. He didn't know why. All he was doing was stating the truth.

After a moment's hesitation, she placed the skillet back onto the cupboard. "Thank you."

He dipped his chin in acknowledgement. He wasn't sure she truly appreciated how great his sacrifice was, but at least she was grateful.

"Well, I'll give you some privacy."

He glanced back at her when he reached the door. She was slumped against the cupboard, eyes closed and arms wrapped around her waist. Realization struck him – he'd frightened her. His own wife was afraid of him.

The thought bothered him as he stepped outside and pulled the door closed. A woman shouldn't be afraid of her husband, even if they'd just met. The last thing he wanted was for her to be scared of him.

He pondered the problem as he walked across the yard towards the barn, Brutus trotting along beside him. Somehow, he'd need to reassure her. If he was going to enjoy the pleasures of the marriage bed tomorrow, she needed to trust him.

But how was he going to get her to do that?

~ ~ ~

It took Gabriel the whole half hour he spent getting the chickens, Fred, Jed and Goat safely away for the night to think of a way to reassure Grace of his trustworthiness. He finally came up with a plan, of sorts, when he remembered something his older sister, Almira, had once told him.

"Gabriel," she'd said, after catching him trying to sneak off with a cookie from the batch she'd just baked, "do you know what women like most in a man?"

He hadn't really cared, being only twelve at the time, but since she was standing between him and a cinnamon cookie, he'd paid attention anyway.

"No."

"Honesty. We don't like cheating and stealing and lying and sneaking around. We like to know where we stand."

He'd given that a good five seconds of thought before replying, "In that case, I'd honestly like a cookie. May I have one?"

She hadn't let him keep the cookie, but the lesson had somehow stuck.

He would be honest with Grace, let her know where she stood. Maybe he'd get lucky and it would reassure her enough to change her mind about consummating the marriage tonight. Couldn't hurt to try.

When he returned to the house, Grace was sitting in his bed, her legs under the bedcovers, a book held up in front of her.

He stood still, his eyes drifting over her. Truth was, she was every bit as covered up as she had been when she was wearing her daytime clothes, and yet it was somehow different. Swallowing, he turned away to close the door after

Brutus had padded inside. His plan to be honest with her wouldn't work if he stood there ogling her like the uncouth brute she thought him.

He sincerely hoped she'd be ready soon if she was going to insist on wearing the not at all revealing nightgown and robe though. There was lace, and a hint of ruffles. The robe was light blue. And the nightgown was pink. *Pink.*

"Do the chickens sleep in the coop?"

He glanced back at her. She'd lowered her book to her lap, revealing more of the pink frilly nightgown. Was that a *ribbon*?

"Uh, yeah, they do. Foxes sometimes come round here. They'd love to get at my chickens."

"Do foxes attack horses and goats?"

"Not the horses, although what with them being predators and all, Fred and Jed get nervous if they're around. A big enough one might go for Goat, though they'd be taking their lives in their hands if they did. She'll charge anything if she feels threatened. Or thinks she can get away with it. But there are wolves and coyotes and bears that would take a goat and maybe even a horse. Have to be careful of those."

He was facing away from her as he spoke, removing his jacket and hat to hang on the coat stand by the door. So it was only when he turned round that he saw her staring at him with eyes like saucers.

"B-bears and wolves?" She looked at the window as if expecting one to burst in at any moment.

He rushed to reassure her. "I don't see them very often and they hardly ever go after people. You're safe here. It ain't nothing to worry about."

51

She looked far from reassured, continuing to stare at the window. If a wolf howled in the distance at that moment, as they did on occasion, she'd probably hit the roof. Or maybe she'd run into his arms. He'd be fine with that.

He spotted the skillet she'd used to keep him at bay earlier, on a shelf above the cupboard. Grace was a woman who would defend herself, if she felt threatened. If he was going to make her feel more secure, maybe he needed to help her do that.

"You know how to use a gun?"

She moved her eyes back to him and shook her head. "My father owns a revolver, but he keeps it locked in a box in his bedroom. I don't think he's used it since he bought it."

"Well, tomorrow I'll teach you how to shoot. That way, when I'm not around, you can defend yourself."

She chewed at her lip. They were enticing, her lips. Full and plump and perfect for kissing.

"I wouldn't want to hurt anything."

His gaze snapped back to her eyes. What were they talking about? *Teaching her to shoot.* Oh yes.

"Mostly, with bears and other animals, you'll just need to fire over their heads and they'll run. The noise scares them."

She smiled slightly. "It would probably scare me too."

"You'll be all right, once I've taught you to handle a gun." He looked down at the floor, scuffing his boot on the wood. Honesty wasn't something that came naturally to him. "Look, I reckon this all must be hard for you and I don't blame you for being nervous and all. But I just want you to know that you're safe with me. I won't do anything to hurt you. I mean, yes, we are gonna be intimate, although not right now if you're not ready, but I promise I'll be gentle. It might hurt a bit to begin with, but that's natural." This wasn't the direction he'd meant to take with his little speech, but he was being honest and women liked honesty. "I mean, it won't be unpleasant. You might even like it. So... so you don't have to be scared. I just wanted you to know that."

There, that wasn't so bad.

He raised his gaze to gauge her reaction to his reassurances. She was staring at him, her eyes wide. She didn't look particularly reassured. Was there such a thing as being too honest? Should he say something else?

"Anyway, um, that's the honest truth. So you're all right now, aren't you?"

She continued to stare wordlessly at him.

He rubbed the back of his neck. "Okay then. Well..." He nodded, pleased he'd cleared the air between them. "You can carry on with your book, if you like."

He spat the gob of tobacco in his cheek into the spittoon by the stove, took a drink from the cup of water he'd left on the table earlier, then walked over to the bed. Sitting on the end, he began to pull off one boot.

"What are you doing?"

He looked back at her. Her eyes were still round.

"I'm getting ready for bed." Which he'd have thought was obvious.

"And where are you going to sleep?"

"In the bed." Which was even more obvious. Where else would he sleep?

"With *me*?"

53

This was possibly the most bewildering conversation he'd ever had. "Unless you plan on sleeping elsewhere."

He didn't think it was possible for her eyes to get any larger, but she proved him wrong.

Throwing her book aside, she grasped the cover and jerked it up to her chin. "You said you didn't expect us to do that!"

"I don't, not right now, if you don't want to." He couldn't deny he was hoping she'd change her mind once he got in beside her. "But I've got to sleep."

She clutched the covers in front of her like a shield. "Not here you don't."

There was that look again. She was afraid of him.

"Grace, I just told you, you have nothing to fear from me. But this is the only place I've got to sleep."

"We'd be in bed together! What if you can't control yourself? Men are like that. They have... urges. You might get urges!"

He sighed. "Yes, I have urges, but any man who claims he can't control himself with a woman is lying. And he ain't much of a man either."

She didn't believe him. He could tell she didn't believe him. Mostly by her expression, which wavered between terrified and resolute.

"We can't share a bed, and that's final."

So much for Mrs. Jones' idea that God would bring him the perfect wife. The perfect wife would be welcoming him with open arms. Right now, he wasn't sure how things with Grace could get any worse.

He huffed out a frustrated breath, lifting his hands to

either side. "Then where am I supposed to sleep?"

"I don't know, but not in here."

"Not in the bed?"

"Not in the room!"

"But there aren't any other rooms!"

"There are two barns."

Apparently, things could indeed get worse.

He gaped at her. She couldn't be serious. "You want me to sleep in the *barn*? Instead of in my own house?"

She pressed her lips together, gripping the cover so tight her knuckles were paling, and nodded.

"I... but... we..."

He looked around the room for inspiration. Finding none, he slumped forward, leaning his elbows onto his knees. Sending for a mail order bride had seemed like such a good idea. Pay for a train ticket and he got a woman to cook, clean, and warm his bed. It had seemed like a good deal, at the time. Back before either of the women had arrived.

Was it like this for every man with a new bride?

"Fine, I'll sleep in the barn rather than in *my own bed*." He jerked his boot back on, not bothering to try to hide his annoyance. "But you'd better get over this ridiculous notion that I need to woo my own wife real soon."

She flinched back when he stomped around the bed, but he was too angry to care. Grabbing the pillow from what should have been his side, he gave her a glare that would leave her in no doubt as to how he felt about the situation, spun away, and stomped to the chest at the end of the bed. He took out a couple of blankets, grabbed the lamp that sat on the table, stomped to the door, and grasped the handle.

It was there that his conscience, such as it was, finally caught up with him.

Sighing, he looked back at her. "Have a good night. If you need anything, you know where to find me."

Without waiting for an answer, he opened the door and called Brutus. He lifted his head from where he was sprawled in front of the cooling stove reluctantly. Gabriel knew just how he felt.

"Come on, boy."

Brutus hauled his huge bulk from the floor, glanced at Grace as if somehow knowing the interruption to his snooze was her fault, and followed Gabriel out the door.

He trudged across the yard with Brutus in tow, muttering under his breath. "That's my bed she's getting all comfortable in. Mine! I mean, I don't mind, what with that being why I brought her here, but I was supposed to be in it with her! Why am I the one being sent to the barn to sleep while she gets to be all comfy and warm?" He reached the barn, yanked open the door, and trudged inside. "Not my fault she's gotten herself all agitated over men's *urges*."

He hung the lamp on a hook beside the door and looked around. He was familiar with every nook and cranny, of course, but the boxes and barrels and tools and shelves transformed into something completely different when he was considering it as a bedroom.

"How in the world am I supposed to get comfortable in here?"

He placed the blankets and pillow on top of a barrel and lit a second lamp. If he was forced to make his bed in there, he was at least going to see what he was sleeping with.

56

He took a fork from the corner, held it in one hand with the lamp in the other, and glanced back at Brutus who was sitting just inside the door.

"Anything runs out, I expect you to get it."

Brutus yawned.

Gabriel sighed and began the task of prodding into all the murky corners of the barn. His dog was hopeless at chasing anything, much less catching it. He could run, he just didn't often see the need.

A sizeable brown rat erupted from the gloom and dashed for the door. Gabriel leaped backwards with a startled cry. Brutus stood, just in time to watch the rat speed past him and into the yard. He took a couple of steps to follow, apparently decided it wasn't worth the effort, and turned back to Gabriel, tail wagging.

"Great, Brutus," he muttered, "that was a real help. I don't know what I'd do without you."

Glad no one had been there to see his embarrassing reaction to the rat, he went back to clearing the rest of the barn. Five minutes later, two more rats had been evicted, and not caught by Brutus, and Gabriel was at least vaguely hopeful he wouldn't be awakened during the night by a rodent chewing on his fingers.

He'd had an idea while prodding around the recesses of the barn to make a mattress from straw, and he grabbed an armful of empty burlap sacks and headed outside. He intended to go straight to the other barn where Fred, Jed and Goat were sleeping, determinedly ignoring the house which, up until a few minutes ago, had been his. But despite his best efforts, his attention still went there.

He'd been short with Grace when he left, he could see that now. Not that she didn't deserve it. He'd be happily tucked up in bed right now if it wasn't for her. But still, he had snapped at her.

Not sure what he intended to do, he crept up the steps to the porch and peered through the window closest to the bed. The curtains were drawn, but there was a gap at the side he could see through.

He drew in a sharp breath when he peeked inside.

Grace was still on the bed, but she was no longer reading. Her knees drawn up to her chest and arms wrapped around them, she was crying.

It was her own fault, he told himself. She'd thrown him out of his house. He could be in there right now, comforting her, but she didn't want him. Instead she was crying, alone. She had only herself to blame.

So why did he feel so guilty?

The long sigh he let out fogged the window pane. Much as he wanted to hold on to his righteous anger, it seemed determined to fade at the sight of his sobbing wife. Had he made her cry? Even though he couldn't for the life of him think what he'd done, it was possible.

He watched her for half a minute until he couldn't bear the sight any longer and slumped back against the wall of the house, rubbing one hand down his face. He could still hear her muffled sobs and the sound tore at his chest. What was he supposed to do now?

He looked at the door away to his left. He could go in there and try to comfort her somehow, although all his attempts thus far to make her feel better about being his wife had been unmitigated failures. He simply didn't know what to say to convince her she was safe with him. And chances were, if he did go in there now he'd only make things worse, maybe even embarrass her that he'd caught her crying. Then there was the whole spying on her through the window, which would give her even more reason to not trust him.

All things considered, going in there would be a bad idea.

Sighing, he gently pressed his palm to the window and peeked inside again. She was still huddled into herself, but he couldn't hear her sobs anymore.

"Please don't cry, Grace," he whispered.

He stood there for a few seconds then turned and headed for the barn, the lingering feeling that he was guilty of something annoying him no end.

~ ~ ~

Grace pulled her handkerchief from her sleeve and blew her nose, grateful she'd finally stopped crying.

She felt as if those tears had been building since she'd left her father at the train station in New York. Right until the moment she stepped onto the train, she'd waited for him to ask her to stay. If he had, she would have. But he didn't.

She wasn't even sure if he'd been sad she was leaving. She'd always been closer to her mother than her father, but she'd never doubted he loved her until that day at the train station a week ago when he said goodbye to his only daughter, his only child, and didn't even once ask her to stay.

Then there was the long, uncomfortable, noisy,

exhausting journey during which she'd barely had a moment when there weren't others around her.

And now here she was with a man she didn't know, scared and alone. And the moment Gabriel had left, she'd burst into tears.

"Why am I here, Lord?" she whispered, dabbing at her burning eyes. "Is this really where I'm supposed to be? Is Gabriel really the man You wanted me to marry?" She sighed and looked at the door. "I thought he'd be more... more... I don't know. I just wanted him to care about how I feel. I want *someone* to care how I feel." She sniffed as pain bloomed in her chest and the tears threatened to resume. "Am I being foolish to want love? Is shelter and provision all I can expect from marriage? I wish Mama hadn't gone to be with You. She wouldn't have cared that I hadn't married by now. She would have understood."

When tears began to roll down her cheeks again, she clamped her handkerchief over her eyes, squeezing them shut and shaking her head. Crying all night wouldn't help her at all. She was here now, so she'd just have to make the best of it. She could do that.

She retreated into making a mental list, her usual method for calming herself when her emotions threatened to drown her.

This one was titled, 'Good Things About Being in California and Married to Gabriel.'

1) Felicia wasn't there to make snide remarks about Grace's attire or size or lack of male attention. That alone might have been worth crossing the country for.

2) The scenery, with the mountains behind and the

valley stretched out in front, was stunning.

3) She liked animals so she was looking forward to getting to know Brutus and the horses and Goat and the chickens.

4) The town seemed nice. Maybe she'd make some friends.

5) The house was small and lacking in basic amenities, but it had a certain cozy charm.

6) Felicia wasn't there. Being an extra good reason, it deserved two spots in the list.

7) Maybe she'd get to taste Mrs. Goodwin's remarkable cooking again.

8) Gabriel...

She wasn't yet sure if he belonged on the list of good reasons about being there.

He was decidedly rough, and he had no idea how to treat a lady. He seemed to lack any sensitivity whatsoever and the chewing tobacco was downright disgusting. That definitely needed to go. His manners were, well, missing. And the way he ogled her bordered on rudeness, even if, as her husband, it could be argued that he had the right. His beard and hair needed trimming and his clothing didn't even come close to being within screaming distance of stylish. He'd exaggerated his 'successful' claim grossly, if the house was anything to go by.

All in all, she couldn't think of one thing to commend him to her good things list.

And yet, there was something about him, although what it was she couldn't put her finger on. Maybe, with work, some of his worst qualities could be reformed.

61

She wiped at her eyes and swallowed the rest of her tears. She wouldn't give up yet. She'd only just arrived. She was tired and emotionally exhausted.

Things would get better. They had to.

She picked up her Bible and opened it. God's word was always a comfort, and she needed the comfort only God could give her more than ever.

With a deep sigh, she settled back into the pillows and began to read.

It was then that she heard the sound of scratching.

~ ~ ~

Gabriel lay back on the blanket and stared at the ceiling. After a while, he sat up, pounded at one of the straw-stuffed sacks beneath him until it was a less uncomfortable shape, and lay down again.

Frowning, he scratched at an itch at the back of his neck. Even with a blanket between him and the rough burlap, he still felt as if it was irritating his skin. If he'd been staying more than one night, he would have needed an extra layer beneath him. But since he would only be sleeping in the barn for a single night and he didn't want to disturb Grace by going back to the house, he could put up with it for now. Also, he couldn't be bothered to get up again.

Brutus briefly opened an eye to look at him from where he was curled on a pile of hay Gabriel had brought in for him. When nothing interesting presented itself, he went back to sleep. It took somewhat longer for Gabriel to relax enough to drift off.

He wasn't sure how long he'd been dozing when soft footsteps outside roused him. The door to the barn inched open and light spilled in.

He pushed his hand beneath his pillow to grasp his revolver, letting it go again when Grace stepped inside, holding a lamp in front of her.

Finally, she'd come to her senses.

He sat up. "You all right?"

She jumped, seeming startled that he was awake. "I... uh... yes. I'm just... um..." She puffed out a breath. "There are noises in the house. It's unnerving."

He shrugged one shoulder. "Probably just the rats."

Her jaw tensed. "There are rats in the house?"

"Not in. Under."

She didn't appear overly reassured by the distinction. "Can they get inside?"

"No, I sealed all the holes they could get in by." So that was why she was here. He'd take whatever he could get. "But I can see you're afraid, so I'll come on back in and make sure you're safe and..."

Her eyes narrowed. "You will do no such thing." She moved her gaze to the dog and patted her thigh with one hand. "Brutus, come here boy."

Brutus lifted his head and blinked sleepily at her.

"Come on," she said, patting again. "I'll give you a treat inside."

Brutus, traitor that he was, hauled himself to his feet and plodded towards her.

Gabriel's mouth dropped open. "You're taking the dog instead of me?"

63

She lifted her chin. "I certainly am. I trust *him* to keep his paws to himself." She spun on her heel and walked out, Brutus following.

Gabriel watched her pull the barn door shut, his mouth still hanging open. A few seconds later, he heard the door to the house open and close.

Closing his mouth, he flopped back onto his makeshift bed and stared into the gloomy rafters above him.

"Where did I go wrong?"

CHAPTER 4

The moment she woke, Grace knew something was wrong.

Someone was in her bedroom.

She gasped in a breath with a jolt, her eyes springing open. Her panicked gaze darted around the room, finally coming to rest on a man standing by the stove.

He nodded to her. "Morning."

Gabriel. Her husband. She was married.

Oh.

She tugged the bedcovers up to her chest, only slightly less afraid than when she'd thought a stranger was in her room. "What are you doing in here?"

"Needed coffee." He raised the tin cup in his hand as evidence. "You may have had me sleeping out in the barn all night, but I miss my morning coffee for no man. Or woman."

Ever so slightly, she relaxed. "Oh, yes. Sorry."

She pushed herself up the pillows and rubbed her eyes. Brutus padded over to her, his tail wagging, and she reached out to ruffle his head.

"Did you sleep well?"

Gabriel stared at her as if she'd lost her mind. "I slept in the barn on sacks stuffed with straw. Alone. Without a wife or a dog. How do you think I slept?"

A small amount of guilt prodded at her. It disappeared when she remembered how he'd all but accosted her when they'd known each other for barely three hours.

"I'm guessing you slept well in my bed," he went on, "seeing as it took you a good fifteen minutes to wake up after I came in." He took a sip of his coffee and grimaced for a moment.

Fifteen minutes? He could have done anything to her in fifteen minutes. Although he hadn't, which was reassuring, she had to concede. And he didn't look like he was imminently likely to accost her again.

She reached for her robe which she'd left draped over the foot of the bed. "I suppose I must have been tired from the journey."

She tried to ignore the way he watched her as she pulled on her robe, doing her best to stay covered to the fullest possible extent.

"Would you like some coffee?" he said as she stood. "Made a fresh pot while you were sleeping."

"Thank you."

She hesitated for a moment then walked over to him. He was her husband. It wouldn't do to be constantly afraid of him. Besides, if he tried anything, she'd just grab the skillet again.

He poured her a cup from the pot and handed it to her. She gave it a wary sniff, took a sip, and immediately regretted it.

"Something wrong?" he said.

Her mouth felt like it was melting. "How can you drink that?"

"What's wrong with it? I like it strong." He took several mouthfuls, to prove his point.

She handed the cup back to him. "That's not merely strong, it's caustic. How is it not eating through the cup?"

Rolling his eyes, he emptied her cup into his own and carried it to the table. "Suit yourself."

As he muttered something about "over-sensitive women", she went to one of her trunks and rummaged inside, pulling out a large paper bag.

"What's that?" he said from his seat at the table.

She walked to the stove and placed the bag on the cupboard beside it. "This is proper coffee." She gave him a look. "Suitable for over-sensitive women."

The corner of his mouth twitched in what might have been a smile, but he said nothing.

She was intensely aware of his eyes on her as she set about grinding the roasted beans, and she wished she could get dressed. But to get dressed would require her to first get *un*dressed, something that wasn't happening until he was well out of the house.

"What are we doing today?" she said as she worked.

"If you're feeling better, I figured I could show you around the place more, teach you what needs doing when I'm not here. And I can teach you how to shoot, like I said."

The idea of using a gun made her nervous, but she hadn't forgotten about the wolves and bears and coyotes he'd told her about the previous evening. "That sounds good."

"So how are you feeling this morning?"

She glanced back at him. He was sipping his awful coffee, watching her over the rim of his cup. He probably thought he was being casual enough for her not to suspect any ulterior motive to the question. He was wrong.

"I'm feeling a little better, thank you."

"Well rested?"

"Still a little tired, but better than yesterday."

There was a pause that stretched into a lengthy silence. Gabriel continued to drink his coffee while she finished grinding the beans, poured over the hot water, and went to make the bed. The smell of real coffee drifted from the pot. Brutus stood and stretched his nose towards it.

"Sorry, it's not for you," Grace said, returning to the stove and ruffling his ears.

She strained the beans twice, set them aside to reuse later, and poured two cups.

Gabriel eyed the cup she placed in front of him as if it was poisonous. "What's this for?"

"I thought you'd like to try my coffee." She sat down opposite him and took a sip of her own, sighing happily at the taste. It reminded her of home.

He picked up the cup and sniffed at it, much as she'd done with his earlier. "Doesn't smell like real coffee. Doesn't look like it either. Real coffee should look like you can waterproof the roof with it."

She snorted a laugh into her cup. "I prefer to drink mine."

Frowning, he took an experimental sip and rolled it around his mouth before swallowing. His frown disappeared and he took another mouthful.

And there they sat, like a real married couple, drinking their morning coffee at the start of the day. It felt strange but

68

not unpleasant. She could imagine getting used to it eventually.

"I can make breakfast, if you'd like," she said when they'd finished.

A smile touched his lips. "Breakfast would be nice."

"But I need to wash up and dress first." She shifted her gaze pointedly to the door.

He didn't move. "Don't let me stop you."

She huffed a sigh. Was he really that dense? "Gabriel, I know this is your house, but right now I need my privacy. So with all due respect, go away."

He raised his eyebrows. "Go away?"

"Yes. Or do I have to get the skillet again?"

She wasn't sure how he'd react to that, but, to her relief, his lips twitched. It seemed he had something of a sense of humor.

He pushed away from the table and stood. "Well, I reckon I'll go and see to the animals. You need anything, just give me a shout."

He turned and walked to the door, calling Brutus who hauled himself to his feet and plodded after him.

At the door, Gabriel glanced back at her. "Um, if you've a mind to make any more coffee for breakfast, you might as well use yours. Wouldn't make much sense making two different pots."

She hid her smile. "I'll do that."

With a nod, he walked out after Brutus and closed the door behind him.

Laughing quietly, she stood and went to find something not too wrinkled to wear.

At least he liked her coffee.

~ ~ ~

As Gabriel pulled the door shut behind him, he was mildly surprised to find himself smiling. Grace had spirit. He liked that. Granted, that spirit had made him sleep in the barn last night, as much as he'd been able to sleep, but in the long term he could see it making for an interesting, lively marriage.

He wasn't used to women saying their minds, or disagreeing with their men. His own mother had taken care of him, his brothers and sisters and the house without complaint. He couldn't remember her once talking back to his father. Of course, it could have happened away from the prying eyes and ears of their children, but he couldn't quite imagine the mild, gentle woman he knew threatening anyone with a skillet. She certainly wouldn't have punched his father.

He raised a hand to his face where it still hurt to touch and chuckled softly. Grace was like no woman he'd ever met before. If he'd known beforehand what she'd be like, he might have been wary of taking her for his wife. But now he'd met her, frustrating as it was to be forced to sleep in the barn and not exercise his husbandly rights to enjoy the pleasures of the marriage bed, he was intrigued.

And once he did get to take her to bed, which would hopefully be tonight, he imagined it would be an exceedingly enjoyable experience.

Musing on that thought, he headed to the barn.

~ ~ ~

Clean and dressed and feeling much better for it, Grace set about preparing breakfast.

She'd learned to cook from her mother and had even taken advanced cookery lessons from a chef in one of New York's finest hotels, but after tasting Mrs. Goodwin's cooking the previous evening all her confidence in her culinary skills had fled. How the woman managed to create such flavor from the basic ingredients available to her, Grace couldn't fathom. If she'd been able to cook like that, maybe she would have found a husband long ago.

She shook her head at herself as she mixed the batter for the apple pancakes she had planned after checking all the food Gabriel had in his cupboards and down in the root cellar. Her lack of success in finding a husband had nothing to do with her cooking skills. To taste any food she prepared, they would first have had to get past her lack of beauty and her own personal standards, a severely limiting combination of factors.

Still, she imagined Mrs. Goodwin as a young woman had suitors lining up for the hand that could prepare such wonders in the kitchen.

But now Grace was married, she did want her husband to enjoy the food she prepared. So even though the fare would be simple, dictated by the basic nature of the ingredients available to her, she was determined to make it as tasty as possible. She hoped to be able to go into town soon so she could see what spices they stocked in the general store.

Gabriel walked in just as the scrambled eggs were almost done. His eyes flicked down to the pale blue dress she'd bought especially for her new married life, and for a

71

moment she thought he might compliment her on it.

"Something smells real good," he said, hanging his hat on a hook by the door.

She quashed any disappointment that he hadn't mentioned the dress. What had she been expecting?

"It'll be ready soon, if you'd like to wash up."

He looked at his hands, turning them over as if checking they actually needed washing. Shrugging, he walked back outside and she heard water splashing.

Brutus padded over to her, his nose raised to sniff the air.

"Don't worry," she told him, "I made some for you too."

He wagged his tail, his eyes fixed on the food arrayed over the top of the stove to keep warm.

"Which is Brutus' dish?" she asked Gabriel when he returned.

He walked to the cupboard and took out three plates. "He doesn't have a special one. He's happy to eat off any of them."

The spoon stirring the eggs came to a halt. "He eats off the same plates we do?"

Gabriel looked at the plates in his hands. "Uh, yes?"

She'd eaten off those plates the previous evening. It took great effort to keep her horror hidden. "That's not very hygienic."

As if to highlight her point, Brutus lay down and began to lick one paw. Grace suppressed a shudder.

"Hasn't ever done me any harm," Gabriel said.

"All that proves is that God has been looking after you."

"I do wash the dishes afterwards," he said, sounding

somewhat defensive.

"I'm not saying you don't. I'm just suggesting that washing them may not be enough." She failed to keep a slight note of hysteria from her voice when Brutus rolled onto his side and moved on to other, worse parts of his anatomy. "Look what he does with his tongue!"

Gabriel heaved a sigh. "Fine, from now on he'll eat from his own dish."

He replaced one of the plates in the cupboard and pulled out a bowl instead. A desperate urge to scrub every dish in the place raw seized Grace. Maybe she'd do it later, when Gabriel wasn't around. And pray she didn't get ill in the meantime.

She spooned some of the food she'd prepared into the bowl and Gabriel carried it out to the porch, followed by an eager Brutus. She was surprised the dog didn't eat at the table with them. A vision of him sitting on one of the chairs with a napkin tied around his neck made her smile.

Gabriel returned as she was dishing out the food and he took the plate she piled high with eggs, ham and pancakes to the table.

"That all you're having?" he said when she followed with her own plate of eggs, a little ham, and no pancakes.

Embarrassed, she placed the plate onto the table and sat, not looking at him. "I'm not very hungry."

"A bird would eat more than that. This isn't your fancy house with servants doing everything for you. You need to keep up your strength." He was still standing, frowning down at her.

"For your information," she said indignantly, "I did my

73

share of the work at home."

"And how did you manage that, if that's all you ate?" He reached for her plate. "At least let me get you some pancakes."

She grabbed the plate and pulled it from his grasp. "It's enough."

"It's not! I won't have you dropping from exhaustion because you haven't eaten hardly anything."

"I'm not going to drop from exhaustion. In case you hadn't noticed, I'm not exactly a waif!" She turned away angrily as tears burned at her eyes. She hated it when she couldn't control her emotions. It was humiliating.

There were several seconds of silence before he spoke. "Please don't cry." When she didn't answer, he walked around in front of her and leaned down to look into her face. "What's wrong?"

She swiped at her eyes. "Nothing's wrong. I'm just trying to get thinner, that's all."

He blinked, his gaze lowering to her body. "Why in the world would you want to get thinner?"

She stared at him, astonished. She would have thought he was being sarcastic, if he hadn't looked so completely bewildered.

"Because I'm fat."

"*Fat*?!" He straightened, his eyes opening wide. "Who told you that?"

Was he really going to make her talk about this? "No one, exactly, in those words. Although my stepmother hints at it all the time." She spread out her arms. "But look at me. I'm just bigger than everyone else."

He planted his hands on his hips. "Grace Silversmith, you are the perfect size. There's nothing worse than trying to hold a bony, skinny woman who's all sharp edges and looks like she'll break if you squeeze too hard. A man wants a woman in his arms he can feel, who's all soft and round and..." He stopped, his neck bobbing as he swallowed. "Anyway, I don't want you getting one bit smaller than you are."

She watched, silent and open-mouthed, as he picked up her plate, carried it to the stove and piled it with more ham and pancakes.

When he returned to the table, he placed it in front of her and sat. "Eat up," he said, waving his fork at her food. "We've got a lot to do today."

She looked down at her full plate then back at Gabriel who was stuffing a forkful of eggs into his mouth.

They hadn't said the blessing, but she was sure God wouldn't mind this once. So she picked up her knife and fork, silently thanked Him for the food and her husband, and began to eat with a smile on her face.

She didn't even mind anymore that Brutus had used the plate before her.

CHAPTER 5

Grace gingerly held the revolver away from her, hands as far from the trigger as they could get. She harbored a small irrational fear that it would go off by itself if she moved too much.

Across the yard, Gabriel finished setting up several rusty tin cans along a plank of wood supported on each end by an upturned bucket and walked back to her. She held the gun out to him, barrel pointed at the ground.

"It won't bite you," he said, taking the revolver from her.

"It's not biting that worries me. It's the bullets coming out of the end."

He opened it to show the empty chambers to her. "No bullets yet, see?"

"Well, now you tell me." An empty gun wasn't as scary as a loaded one.

"That's your first lesson. Treat an unloaded gun with as much respect as a loaded one, just in case."

"In case of what?" She eyed the revolver warily, fully prepared to be afraid of it even when empty.

"In case it isn't unloaded. The rule is, all guns are loaded."

Now she was confused. "But you just said it's not

loaded."

"Yes, but it might be."

"Well, is it or isn't it?"

"It isn't, but you should always treat it as if it is until you know for certain that it isn't by checking the cylinder, like I just did."

It took her a moment to sort that out in her mind before it made sense. "And if it is really empty? Is it still dangerous?"

"Only if someone hits you with it." His lips curved up slightly. "And I'd appreciate it if you didn't ever do that, by the way."

At least he could joke about her punching him the night before. She wasn't sure how he'd feel about that today. Not that she regretted what she'd done, of course.

She pretended to consider his request. "I can't promise anything."

"Well can you at least promise not to shoot me?"

She pursed her lips. "I'll think about it."

"Fair enough." He held the gun out to her. "We'll start with how to hold and aim it."

She took the gun back with far less apprehension, now she knew there were no bullets inside.

"Now," he said, "there are three rules when handling a gun. One, all guns are loaded."

"Even the ones that aren't," she said, still a little unsure about how that worked.

"Right. Two, you don't ever point a gun at anything or anyone you aren't willing to shoot."

She looked at the gun in her hands. "But I don't want to

77

shoot anything or anyone, so why do I need to learn how?"

Taking hold of her shoulders, he looked into her eyes. "Because we're on our own out here and I need to know you'll be able to protect yourself when I'm not around."

Sighing, she nodded. Even though she didn't like it, she understood.

His hands slipped from her shoulders. "Okay. The third rule is, don't ever shoot at anything without knowing what's behind it."

Finally, a rule she wasn't confused about. "Got it."

"Good. Now, hold the gun in your right hand, pointed at the ground, index finger inside the trigger guard but not on the trigger, and turn side on to the target."

She did as she was instructed, wrapping her hand around the stock and looking along her right shoulder. So intent was she on the row of cans fifteen feet away that she didn't notice Gabriel had moved until he was standing right behind her, his chest lightly touching her back.

His breath brushed over the side of her neck as he spoke. "Now pick your target, keep your arm straight, and raise the gun slowly. Keep your eyes on the target. Don't pull the trigger."

Swallowing against her suddenly dry mouth, she raised her arm until the gun was pointed at the can she'd chosen.

He slid his fingers along her arm to her wrist. "That's good, nice and straight, shoulder lined up with your hand. Try not to let the gun shake. There's nothing to be afraid of."

Her trembling hand had nothing to do with fear and everything to do with his proximity doing annoying things to her heartbeat, but she wasn't about to tell him that. With a supreme effort, she got her limbs more or less under control and the muzzle of the gun steadied.

"That's real good. You can put your arm down now."

She expected him to move away as she lowered her arm. He didn't.

"Now do that again, but this time, keep moving the gun up through the target, without stopping."

Trying to ignore his closeness, she repeated the action, this time keeping the gun moving until it had passed through the tin can.

"That's good. We'll do it a few more times until you have that down, then you can try pulling the trigger."

She lowered the gun to her side again. "Is there a reason you're standing so close to me?"

"Just making sure you're getting it right."

She could hear the smile in his voice.

"Why do I not believe you?"

The vibrations from his chuckle traveled from his chest down into her spine. "Can't blame a man for trying."

As he stepped back, the thought came to her that she shouldn't have said anything. She ignored it.

Gabriel had her practicing first the basic movement of the gun and then dry firing using spent cartridges for a good twenty minutes before he deemed her ready to fire an actual live round.

"Now when you fire this," he said, loading a single bullet into the gun, "it's going to be loud and you'll feel it kick back through your arm. But if you do it exactly how you've been doing it so far, you'll be just fine."

He held the gun out to her.

After a moment's hesitation, she took it, listing the rules in her mind to keep herself calm.

1) All guns are loaded. Including the one she held, for real this time.

2) Never point a gun at anything or anyone you aren't willing to shoot. So for now, only the tin cans.

3) Don't ever shoot at anything without knowing what's behind it.

She leaned slightly to one side to check behind the row of cans.

"Now just raise your arm slowly, like you've been doing, and pull the trigger when the muzzle is pointing at the can."

She drew in a deep breath, ignored the thudding of her heart, and slowly raised her arm, eyes fastened on the can she'd been using as her target.

"Don't hold your breath."

She glanced at him in annoyance. "I wasn't holding my breath." She had been, but only for a few seconds.

He gave her a look that said he didn't believe her.

Returning her focus to the can, she began again. Breathe in, breathe out, raise arm slowly, pull trigger.

The gunshot was louder than she was expecting and she yelped and stumbled back with the recoil, almost falling before Gabriel's arms wrapped around her from behind. She gasped in a breath, her heart pounding.

The first thought that entered her mind was that she never wanted to fire a gun again.

The second was that being held by a man she wasn't related to felt rather nice.

80

"Thank you," she said, when she'd gathered herself enough to speak.

"You're welcome."

There were a few moments of silence before she spoke again. "You can let go now."

"You sure?" There was a smile in his voice.

"Positive."

He didn't let go. "I wouldn't want you to fall or swoon or anything."

She had the strongest urge to smile, although she didn't. "May I remind you that I am holding a gun and haven't yet promised not to shoot you?"

He released her with a chuckle. "That wasn't bad, apart from the end."

"Did I hit anything?" She turned to look at the cans. To her disappointment, they were all still firmly in place.

"I reckon the ground will be hurting for a while."

"I hit the *ground*?" Her shoulders slumped.

"You pulled the trigger too soon. Leave it just a mite longer next time, until the muzzle is covering the can."

She groaned. "Next time? I have to do it again?"

"Not much point in knowing how to shoot if you can't hit anything."

Much as she hated to admit it, he was right, she did need to know how to defend herself. At least the second time she'd know what to expect and wouldn't be so startled.

"Good morning!"

Grace turned at the unexpected voice to see a man approaching on horseback. He smiled and waved.

"What's he doing here?" Gabriel muttered, looking none

81

too pleased to see the man, whoever he was.

Brutus lifted his bulk up from the sunny porch where he'd been snoozing and stalked down the steps to the yard, eyeing the stranger warily.

"Good morning," the man repeated, bringing his horse to a halt in the middle of the yard. "Mr. Silversmith. Ma'am." He tipped his hat towards Grace. "Lovely day, isn't it?"

Brutus came to stand at Gabriel's side and the man's horse snorted a breath, taking a step back. He laid a hand on its neck to calm it.

"Something I can do for you, Fowler?" Gabriel said, his tone cold.

"I heard you'd got yourself a wife and just thought I'd come and see if you'd reconsidered our offer, in light of your new circumstances. And may I say, a lovely wife she is too." He nodded at Grace, although his smile contained no warmth.

For some reason she couldn't put her finger on, he made her uneasy.

Gabriel stepped in front of her. "I haven't reconsidered, because the answer will always be no."

The smile on Mr. Fowler's face faltered for a moment. "Are you sure about that? That money would make a world of difference to you and your wife. You could make great improvements to this place. I can't imagine a woman could be happy living here, especially one of obvious refinement such as Mrs. Silversmith." He looked around with an exaggerated expression of sadness and disgust.

Grace had no more appreciation for her new home than she'd had the day before. It was tiny and basic, barely more than a shack. It was, however, *her* shack. Hers and her husband's.

"Thank you for your consideration, Mr. Fowler," she said, "but I like my new home just fine."

Gabriel's head whipped around to stare at her. She didn't think he could have looked more surprised if he'd tried.

Mr. Fowler's narrowed eyes said he didn't believe her for one second. "That's very generous of you, Mrs. Silversmith. I'm not sure I would be quite so forgiving if I were forced to live here. Mr. Silversmith is a fortunate man."

She didn't respond, well acquainted as she was with such backhanded compliments. There was no good way to answer them.

"Anything else you wanted?" Gabriel said.

"I guess not. When you change your mind, you know where to find me." Mr. Fowler touched the brim of his hat to Grace. "Ma'am."

Brutus gave a soft woof as he rode out of the yard and Gabriel placed a hand on his head, watching Mr. Fowler silently until he was a long way off.

Grace went to stand at his side. "Who is he?"

A nerve twitched in his jaw. "Just someone whose employers want to buy my claim. Been trying to convince me to sell for a couple of months now. I don't know how he found out about you."

She watched the distant shape of Mr. Fowler as he rode out of sight behind an outcrop of rock. "I don't like him. He was rude and condescending."

A small smile drifted across Gabriel's face. "Well then,

we agree on one thing, at least."

She smiled. "At least."

"Did you mean that, about liking this place just fine?"

She shrugged and looked around. "I won't deny it's a little basic. Well, very basic. But I think I might learn to like it one day."

He pushed his hands into his pockets, his gaze lowering to the ground. "I'll make it better. Soon as my claim starts producing more, I'll add on a room and get a well dug. Maybe even get some of that indoor plumbing."

In that moment, Grace saw her husband in a new light. Yes, he was rough around the edges, lacked manners, had some disgusting habits, and had not the slightest idea of how to treat a lady. But underneath it all, he cared about what she thought of him and her new home. It was still true that he'd take some work, but it was a start. A good start.

She reached out to touch his arm. "Come on, I need to learn how to shoot, just in case Mr. Fowler comes round again."

Tiny lines crinkled at the corners of his eyes. "Best get you so you can hit something then."

~ ~ ~

By the time they ate supper that evening, Grace looked exhausted.

Gabriel was slightly worried he'd got her doing too much. Despite her sturdy appearance and her insistence otherwise, he knew she had to be used to servants doing the bulk of the work around a house for her. Still, she'd done

84

well.

She'd learned to handle both his revolver and his rifle, and with more practice he was sure she'd eventually be able to hit what she was aiming at. She'd also learned all about taking care of the animals and given the stove a thorough cleaning. He had told her it didn't need it, but she'd insisted so he'd just let her get on with it. He didn't understand women sometimes. Well, most of the time, if he was honest.

As she was tired, he helped her with the cooking, and after supper he offered to clean the dishes by himself while she rested. It wasn't an entirely selfless act on his part since he planned on partaking of the marriage bed that evening, but he was still pleased with himself. He could be a good husband. He understood wives had needs too.

So he washed and dried the dishes alone in the lowering light outside on the porch, whistling softly and thinking about the fun he was going to have teaching Grace about the best part of being married.

By the time he'd finished and carried the pile of clean dishes back inside, he'd been grinning for a good solid ten minutes straight.

The moment he stepped over the threshold, however, his smile faded. Grace lay on the bed fully dressed, curled on her side on top of the bedclothes with her clasped hands tucked beneath her chin. And she was fast asleep.

He placed the dishes on the table and walked over to her. "Grace?"

There was no response.

He repeated her name a little louder, touching her shoulder gently

Still nothing.

Straightening, he stared at his soundly sleeping wife, one hand still stretched towards her as he considered what to do.

He could wake her, he knew. He could wake her and join her in bed and insist she fulfilled her wifely duties. He wouldn't be doing anything wrong. It was his right, as a husband, to enjoy the pleasures of the marriage bed. It said so in the Bible. Well, he wasn't sure of that, but he was pretty sure it said God created men and women to come together in union, or something like that. So it wouldn't be wrong for him to wake her and do what was natural for a husband and wife to do.

Sighing, he dropped his hand to his side. It might not have been wrong, but if he had to convince himself of that, *something* was.

Taking the blanket folded on the end of the bed, he shook it out and draped it over her gently.

"Goodnight, Grace," he whispered.

As he headed for the door, Brutus raised his head from where he lay on the rug beside the stove.

Gabriel considered for a moment, then shook his head. "No, you stay here, Brute. She might need you."

He took the lamp from the table and with a final, regretful glance back at his sleeping wife, walked out the door.

Tomorrow. He'd let her sleep tonight, but tomorrow he was definitely getting back into his own bed.

With his wife in it.

Awake.

CHAPTER 6

Grace felt surprisingly refreshed when she woke the next morning.

She was somewhat confused to find she was lying on top of the bedcovers, albeit with a blanket draped across her. She couldn't remember falling asleep the night before. Had Gabriel put the blanket over her?

Sitting up, she rubbed at her eyes and looked around. Brutus was fast asleep by the stove. Gabriel wasn't in the room. He must have left to sleep in the barn.

She'd been a little nervous at the prospect of sending him out there again. Not that she hadn't planned to, but she'd been anticipating having to argue. And then she must have fallen asleep and he'd gone by himself. Not only that, he'd left Brutus with her.

A sense of peace rolled over her. Underneath the rough exterior, she was beginning to suspect there was a very good man lurking, just as Mrs. Jones had said.

She went through her list of good things about being in California, married to Gabriel, once more.

1) Felicia wasn't there, making snide remarks about Grace's attire or size or lack of male attention.

2) The scenery outside the house, with the mountains

behind and the valley stretched out in front, was the most beautiful she'd ever seen.

3) She liked animals, and she was enjoying getting to know Brutus and the horses and Goat and the chickens. Well, Brutus, the horses and the chickens. Goat scared her a little.

4) The town seemed nice. Maybe she'd make some friends. Gabriel had said at supper that they could travel in today.

5) Gabriel. He was solidly in her list now.

6) The house was small and lacking in basic amenities, but it had a certain cozy charm.

She ran her hand over the blanket Gabriel had placed over her and made a revision, moving him up to fourth. That kind of thoughtfulness definitely deserved an extra place.

Her watch was still in her pocket and she dug it out to find it was just after seven. Time enough to get washed and dressed and maybe even start breakfast before he was up.

She swiveled her feet off the bed, pulled on her shoes, and stood.

As she folded the blanket, she realized she was smiling.

~ ~ ~

The food was cooking on the stove by the time Gabriel walked in. He looked surprised to see Grace up.

"Good morning." She indicated the table. "Have a seat. Breakfast's almost ready."

"Uh, thanks."

She filled a cup from the coffee pot and carried it over to him. "Sorry, but I couldn't work out how to make your roof-waterproofing coffee, so I did mine. You can make your own if you'd like."

He took a sip and shook his head. "No, this will do. No sense in making two pots."

Hiding her smile, she returned to the stove. "Thank you, for last night."

"Last night?"

She kept her eyes on the eggs she was stirring. "Yes. For the blanket and letting me sleep and... everything. I truly appreciate that you did that, and left me alone, and for Brutus."

"I reckoned you needed your rest."

"I did, and I'm grateful. And I want you to know that I also appreciate that you're giving me time before we... you know. I know a lot of men wouldn't think they should have to." She hadn't intended to say it, but now she'd started, it seemed important to get it all out in the open, so they both knew where they stood.

After a few seconds of silence, she glanced back at him.

His eyes moved from her to the bed and then back again. "How much time do you think you're gonna need?"

She bit her lip. "I don't know. I think I'll know when I'm ready though."

There were another few seconds of silence.

She stirred the eggs.

"So... not tonight then?"

"Not tonight, no." She removed the eggs from the heat and turned to face him. "I'm sorry, but this is important to me."

He placed his empty cup down on the table in front of

him and stared at it. "I'm gonna be honest with you, I hadn't figured on having to wait. And I certainly hadn't figured on sleeping in the barn." His chest rose and fell in a sigh. "But I reckon we're going to have the rest of our lives together, so I can wait. Although not for too long, I hope."

She breathed out. "Thank you for understanding."

"I didn't say I understood. Truth is, I can't say as I've ever understood women, no offence intended. But if it's important to you then I reckon, as your husband, it should be important to me too."

To her surprise, her heart did a little flutter. If he kept saying things like that, he was going to move up another place in her list.

He raised his gaze and gave her a small, wistful smile. "But I reckon I ought to get to wooing."

~ ~ ~

Gabriel didn't have the first idea how to woo a woman. Where did a person even start?

He glanced at Grace sitting beside him on the buckboard seat as they drove into town. He still didn't understand why he needed to woo a woman who was already his wife, but if it got him back into his own bed and, more importantly, persuaded her to allow him to bed her, he'd learn how.

He just needed someone to teach him.

"I'm going to be picking up supplies most of the time," he said to Grace as they came to a halt outside the post office in Green Hill Creek's main street. "So I reckon it might be best if you go do whatever you planned to and we meet back here later, if you're all right with that?" *Please say yes, please say yes, please say yes.*

She looked around her, her joy at being there clear on her face.

The moment he'd asked her the evening before if she wanted to go into town, she'd said yes. He supposed she missed having other people around, coming from the big city as she did. It worried him that she might not be happy just having him to talk to most days, but there wasn't anything he could do about that.

"I'm happy to do that," she said. "I want to explore anyway, and do some shopping."

He exhaled, relieved he'd get the time on his own for what he needed to do. "How long do you reckon you'll need?"

She opened her reticule and took out her watch. "It's just past eleven now. Would three hours be too long?"

"Nope. Three hours will be just fine." Plenty of time to pick up the feed for the animals, buy a few other things he had need of, and pay a visit to the one person he was even remotely comfortable talking to about such things as wooing.

"Then I'll meet you back here in three hours."

He waited for her to climb down, bid her goodbye, and got Fred and Jed moving, guiding them towards the church. When he got there he carried on towards the home of Pastor and Mrs. Jones, hoping Mrs. Jones was in. He figured that, as a woman, she'd know all about wooing.

To his relief, she opened the door when he knocked.

"Mr. Silversmith." She looked behind him to the buckboard on the street. "Where's Grace?"

By the worry on her face, he guessed she thought he might have thrown another woman out of his home.

"She said she was going to explore the town and do some shopping. I said I would be picking up feed and such." He swallowed, feeling awkward. "I wanted to talk to you about... things. If you have the time."

She stood back to allow him inside. "Of course. You know you're welcome here any time and Simon and I will help you with anything you need. He's in his study. Did you want to talk to him?"

Gabriel snatched his hat from his head and held it in front of him. "Well, I think maybe you'd know better how to help me, you being a woman and all."

A knowing smile slid onto her face. "Oh, I see. You need *that* kind of help."

Embarrassed, he simply nodded and hoped against hope he was wrong and this *wasn't* going to be the most excruciating conversation of his life.

She led him into the parlor. "May I get you anything to eat or drink?"

"Uh, no ma'am, thank you." He lowered to the edge of the first chair he came to and clutched his hat in his lap.

Mrs. Jones sat on the settee opposite him, appearing markedly more relaxed than he was. "What can I help you with?"

"Well, uh, it's like this. Um. Seeing as you did so well helping me with what to say on the advertisement that got Grace here in the first place, I thought that maybe you'd be able to teach me how to... to woo her."

"Woo?"

"That's what she said. Woo. She wants me to woo her before she'll... um..." Why had he come here? Surely there was an easier way.

"Before she'll...?" Mrs. Jones prompted, when he failed to complete the sentence.

He released a sigh and unpeeled his fingers from his hat. "Before she'll let me sleep in the house. With her."

She looked confused. "Where are you sleeping now?"

"Barn."

Mrs. Jones pressed her lips together and looked at her lap for a few moments before replying. "Oh. Well. Um. Yes. I can certainly help you with wooing."

She thought it was funny. He may not have been very good at reading women, but he could see that much.

"It's not funny."

She gave a delicate snort, covering her mouth with her hand. "Forgive me, I'm not laughing at you, I promise. It's just... the situation is a little funny."

"Only when you're not the one sleeping in the barn."

She nodded, her eyes still dancing with merriment. "I can understand that."

"So can you help me?"

She sat back. "I believe I can."

~ ~ ~

The post office in Green Hill Creek was the smallest Grace had ever seen, but then the town itself was hardly large.

She walked in the door and almost collided with a hammer. The man holding it jerked back with a gasp, snatching the hammer away before it hit her. She lowered her arms, which she'd thrown up to ward off the blow.

"I'm so sorry! Are you all right?" He reached out a hand to steady her.

She pushed a strand of hair back from her eyes and nodded. "Yes, thank you. I was just startled."

"I should probably have waited to fix the doorframe until the post office is closed, but it was quiet and..." He shrugged and smiled. He had the bluest eyes she'd ever seen, a striking contrast to his dark hair. "May I help you?"

She lifted the now slightly crumpled letter in her hand. "I'd like to mail this."

"Of course. Right this way."

She followed him across the small room to where he walked behind the counter and placed the hammer down.

"I don't believe we've met," he said, taking the letter she handed him and smoothing it out. "I'm Adam Emerson, Green Hill Creek's postmaster. And part time bank teller, as you'll discover if you frequent the bank."

"Mrs. Grace Silversmith. It's a pleasure to meet you."

"Mrs. Silversmith? So you're Gabriel Silversmith's new bride?"

"I am, yes."

He took a sheet of stamps from beneath the counter. "Well then, welcome to Green Hill Creek. Have you come from far away?"

"New York City."

"My wife is from New York." He affixed a stamp to the envelope. "She's only been here three months, but she loves it. She says it's so much cleaner and quieter than in the city."

Excitement fluttered through Grace. Another woman from New York would surely understand what she was going through.

"She's certainly right about that. Is she here? I'd very much like to meet her."

"She works at the livery, but I know she'd enjoy meeting you too. If you have time, you should go down there." He pointed to his left. "It's along this street, at the edge of town. Not too far."

She blinked at him, unsure if she'd heard correctly. "Forgive me, but did you say she works at the livery?"

He grinned. "It's a long story."

A story she was now intrigued to hear. Perhaps she'd go and visit Mrs. Emerson after she left the post office. A woman working at a livery. She'd never heard of such a thing.

Mr. Emerson dropped the letter to her father into a canvas sack behind him. "That'll be three cents for the stamp." He took the nickel she gave him and gave her two pennies in exchange. "There are other women here from New York too. I'm sure it won't take you long to feel right at home."

She couldn't help but smile. "Thank you. I think you're right."

~ ~ ~

Parsons' Livery and Sales Stable was a pleasant stroll along Green Hill Creek's main street.

Grace walked through the open front doors and looked around. She'd been in big, busy, bustling liveries in New

95

York plenty of times. This place was nothing like any of them. For one thing, it was quiet. And clean, smelling of nothing more unpleasant than hay. It was also seemingly empty.

She called out into the silence. "Hallo?"

A blonde head popped up above the wall of one of the stalls toward the far end of the building.

"Oh, sorry, I didn't hear you come in." The young woman emerged from the stall and approached Grace with a smile. "What can I do for you?"

For a moment, Grace was slightly taken aback. She'd never seen a woman wearing trousers before. But she had to admit, they looked practical. There were times when struggling to perform certain tasks with her skirts tangling around her legs was intensely frustrating.

"Are you Mrs. Emerson?"

"I am."

"Your husband told me I could find you here. I'm Mrs. Grace Silversmith." She held out her hand.

Mrs. Emerson tugged her leather gloves off and took it. "Oh, Gabriel's new wife?"

There was that word again. *New.* It wasn't the word so much as the way they said it. Grace shrugged it off. They probably simply meant she was newly married and she was just imagining the slight emphasis.

"Yes. Your husband thought I might like to meet you, since we're both from New York. I admit it's a relief to find I'm not the only one. I think I'm still feeling a bit dazed to be here."

Mrs. Emerson laughed. "I know that feeling well."

"Amy? We got a customer?" A man stood at the back

door, a shovel in his hands.

Mrs. Emerson beckoned him over. "George, this is Mrs. Grace Silversmith, Gabriel's new bride. Mrs. Silversmith, this is George Parsons. He owns the livery. Don't call him Mr. Parsons, he hates that."

"Morning." George nodded to her. "Just call me George. Everyone does."

"It's a pleasure to meet you, George."

A woman working in a livery and a man she was calling by his given name as soon as she met him. Grace's day was filling with new experiences.

"Pleasure to meet you too, ma'am."

"I'm going to take a break so Mrs. Silversmith and I can chat," Mrs. Emerson said.

George's eyebrows reached for his gray-sprinkled dark hair. "I seem to recall you took a break an hour ago."

She grinned and patted his arm. "And I know you won't mind me taking another, seeing as you're a nice person."

He rolled his eyes. "Go on then. Not like I can stop you." He tipped his hat to Grace. "Ma'am."

"Don't mind him," Mrs. Emerson said as he walked back outside. "He seems like a grump, but he's really a lovely man." She wrapped her arm around Grace's and led her towards the back doors. "We can sit outside and watch the horses and I'll tell you all about how much you're going to love it here."

~ ~ ~

By the time Grace left the livery, she knew she'd made a

friend. And with Amy's effusive description of the town and her promise to introduce her to the other mail order brides she'd arrived with, she was also beginning to feel like she could truly be part of the community, even living so far out of town.

She spent some time wandering along the main street of Green Hill Creek, drifting in and out of shops, buying a few items she wanted, meeting the local people, and generally enjoying being back in civilization.

Not that she regarded Gabriel's home as uncivilized. Well, not much. But she was glad to be meeting her new neighbors and doing something other than cooking and cleaning and learning how to take care of animals. It wasn't like her shopping trips back in New York, but it was pleasant. She'd brought enough money with her that she would be able to buy anything she needed for the time being without having to ask Gabriel for any.

She eventually reached the hotel at the end of the street and was pleased to find they were serving lunch. After a delicious meal consisting of an inspired combination of Mexican and American food, she wandered back along the street to meet Gabriel.

Right on time, he pulled the buckboard up outside the post office as she arrived. As she placed the bag filled with her purchases behind the seat, he jumped to the ground.

She glanced around her. "Is something wrong?"

He twisted his hands together. "Uh... no. I just thought you might want me to help you up."

It took a moment for it to dawn on her what he meant. "You mean into the buckboard?"

He nodded.

"Oh, um, all right. Yes, thank you." She had no idea what had happened that he would suddenly want to help her, but she wasn't about to refuse.

He looked relieved. "All right then." There were a few seconds of silence. "Um... how do I do that without, um, touching..." He waved his hands in her general direction.

She stifled the urge to laugh. "You may touch my hands. Or my waist, if necessary."

He hooked his thumbs into his pockets, a faint smile playing on his lips. "And you won't punch me?"

"I promise not to punch you, as long as you don't stray from the designated areas."

"As in, waist or hands?"

"As in waist or hands."

He nodded. "Just so I know where I stand. You punch real hard."

"Thank you! That's very kind of you to say."

His brow knotted in bemusement. "I don't know many women as would take that as a compliment."

"Then you haven't met the right women."

A smile replaced his confusion. "I reckon I haven't, until now."

Feeling her cheeks heating, she turned towards the buckboard. She had no idea what had happened to make him so attentive, but she liked it. And she didn't mind at all when he placed his hands on her waist to help her up.

Joining her on the seat, he twisted round to reach behind him and brought forward a posy of yellow wildflowers. "I got these for you. Reckoned you might like them."

99

The slightly awkward way he handed her the flowers, as if he wasn't sure he was doing it right, made her heart melt a little. What in the world had happened to him while they were apart?

"Thank you, they're beautiful. I like them very much."

He nodded, blew out a breath, and set Fred and Jed moving.

"Did you get everything you needed?" he said, guiding the wagon onto a road that Grace recognized from the day she'd arrived.

"Most of it. Mr. Lamb didn't have everything, but he placed a special order for the coffee beans I like. The stores here are remarkably well supplied, considering how far we are from any large towns. I suppose having the railroad run right through town has its advantages."

"I reckon so. I've lived places where it took hours just to get to a store, any store. This is a good place to settle down." He glanced at her then back at the road ahead. "Raise young 'uns."

She looked down at the flowers in her lap. "Yes."

Despite her first impressions of him, perhaps it wasn't such a bad thing being married to Gabriel, and being the future mother of his children. Its appeal was certainly growing.

As they left the town behind, he reached inside his jacket and pulled out the leather pouch containing his chewing tobacco. Grace grimaced at the smell that wafted out when he opened it. If she was going to succumb to any kind of intimacy with him, however appealing that might become, she was going to have to deal with this first.

She twisted round to search her bag. "I bought something for you."

"You did?" He withdrew his fingers from the pouch to take the small square tin she handed to him. "What is it?"

"Spruce chewing gum. I didn't know if I'd be able to find it, but Mr. Lamb had it in his store. I thought you could use it instead of that." She nodded at the pouch in his hand.

He followed her gaze. "Why would I do that?"

She again went over the arguments she'd prepared in her mind. She wasn't at all sure how this would go down with him.

"I would like you to stop using chewing tobacco." She'd decided being straightforward about it would be best.

A look of confusion crossed his face. "Why?"

"Because it smells awful and looks awful, but, more importantly, it's dangerous." Clear and concise, so he'd see she was right.

"Dangerous? Where'd you get a ridiculous notion like that?" He shook his head, holding out the tin of gum to her. "Here. I'm obliged, but I don't need it."

She pushed the tin back to him. "I've read about it. Research has been done. Many doctors are saying that tobacco, in whatever form, has a bad effect on the body. It causes all kinds of illness and cancer."

He placed the tin on the seat between them. "I don't believe it. I've never had any trouble with it."

"That doesn't mean you won't. Haven't you ever known anyone who got sick from chewing tobacco?"

He looked ahead of them, pressing his lips together.

"My father used to smoke cigars," she went on,

determined to get him to see her point. "My mother finally got him to stop when I was fifteen. It was hard for him, but he did it, and he felt a lot better for it once he had. He had a cough that disappeared and he said he felt like he had more energy and he..."

"I ain't stopping, and that's final." He still wasn't looking at her.

"But..."

He rounded on her angrily. "You've been here less than three days and so far I've been pushed out of my own bed, can't touch my own wife, can't even sleep in the house, and now you want me to stop chewing? Well I ain't doing it, so you'll just have to get used to it!" He shoved the tin of chewing gum towards her and turned back to scowl at the track ahead of them.

For a few moments she couldn't do anything but stare at him. She wasn't used to people simply dismissing her outright.

Slowly, however, anger replaced her shock. "Chewing tobacco is a disgusting habit. And no matter what you think, it's unhealthy. And furthermore, if you think you are getting anywhere near me while your breath smells like a cesspit, you are gravely mistaken!"

He glanced at her and for a moment she thought he was going to argue further, but instead he clamped his mouth shut and looked forward, brows bunched together.

Folding her arms, she whirled away from him and frowned out across the fields of gently waving wheat.

Everything had been going so well. She'd been sure that, once she explained the dangers of chewing tobacco, he'd

102

understand and agree with her. Why did he have to be so stubborn?

And what was she going to do now?

CHAPTER 7

Gabriel sat down on the straw mattress in the barn and huffed out a frustrated breath.

So much for trying to woo his wife. Grace didn't need to be wooed, she needed some sense talked into her.

He'd thought things were looking up between them, but now he wasn't sure they could get any worse. They'd barely spoken since the ride home. Grace had added some kind of spice she'd bought in town to their supper of vegetable stew and it had been delicious, but she hadn't said one word while they ate it. Although neither had he.

The nerve of the woman, asking him to give up his tobacco. He'd been chewing tobacco since he was fifteen years old and it hadn't ever done him any harm.

All right, so he'd lost that one tooth at the back on the side where he usually held it, but that could have been anything. Lots of people had missing teeth.

And yes, his uncle had developed a tumor in his throat that eventually killed him at the age of forty-nine, but there was no proof that was caused by his chewing tobacco. Even folks who didn't use tobacco got cancer.

Without thinking, he took his tobacco pouch from his pocket, his hands absently going through the motions.

And what was he still doing here in the barn? This was the third night he'd been married. Who didn't get to sleep with their wife for three nights? And how long was this going to go on for? She had no right to tell him what to do when he wasn't even sleeping in his own bed.

He glanced towards the barn door, only then noticing the lamplight glinting on something resting near the end of his makeshift bed. It was the tin of spruce gum. He hadn't touched the thing since Grace had tried to give it to him on the way home. She must have put it on his bed when he wasn't looking.

He leaned over to pick it up, turning the small tin box over and over in his hand. Maybe she was trying to help him, but he didn't need help. He'd run his life perfectly well before she arrived. Why couldn't she just be like other wives and do what her husband said?

Although, since she'd bought the stuff, it wouldn't do any harm to try it.

He returned the pinch of tobacco to the pouch and closed it.

He'd try a piece of the gum first. Then he'd have the tobacco.

CHAPTER 8

Grace was hoping that Gabriel would work through his anger with her for asking him to stop chewing tobacco during the night. The moment he entered the house the following morning, however, her hopes were dashed.

It wasn't as if he walked around radiating a permanent glow of joy, but in her admittedly limited experience of him, he did normally seem fairly content. Not this morning though.

He muttered, "Morning," and sat at the table with barely a glance in her direction.

Brutus raised his head from his spot by the stove, apparently decided Gabriel wasn't in the mood for any interaction, and went back to sleep.

Grace poured a cup of coffee and set it on the table. "Good morning. Did you sleep well?"

His only response was a silent shrug.

Sighing, she returned to the breakfast cooking on the stove.

They ate in an uncomfortable silence, Grace wondering the entire time if she should say something. On the one hand, she wanted to talk to him. It was only now, as they sat quiet and unspeaking, that she appreciated how much she enjoyed their conversations. But on the other hand, his surliness annoyed her.

She hadn't been wrong to ask him to stop chewing tobacco. All she'd done was care enough to want him to stop doing something that was hurting him. She wouldn't apologize for that.

Yes, it was also for her benefit. Seeing him spit out the vile stuff made her feel positively ill. And the smell, well, there was no way she could kiss a man who smelled like that. But wasn't her comfort important too?

So they sat in silence, eating the fried potatoes she'd made for breakfast while determinedly not acknowledging each other's presence.

It was so quiet that Grace almost jumped out of her skin when Gabriel pushed his empty plate away and spoke. "I'll be going up to my claim today so I'll need you to take care of the animals. I've fed them now, but they'll need another feeding around five. And Goat will need milking again."

"All right." She could do that. Probably.

"I might not be back until late."

"I'll keep your supper warm."

He stared at his hands resting on the table. "If I don't come back tonight, it means I've decided to stay up there and I'll be back tomorrow."

Her stomach lurched. "You... you're going to leave me here on my own at night?"

Even though he slept in the barn, his presence made her feel safe. The prospect of being left all by herself terrified her. She'd never been on her own at night.

His eyes remained on his hands. "You'll be fine. I'll leave

Brutus here with you and you know how to shoot now."

"I know, but... but what if something happens? Please don't leave me alone."

His shoulders rose and fell in a sigh and for a moment she thought he might relent. But then his hands tightened into fists. "You don't need me here. You can look after yourself just fine. Pretty sure you don't want me here either."

He stood abruptly and strode out the door. A minute later, he rode away on Jed.

Suddenly realizing he was being left behind, Brutus stood and trotted to the door. He whined and looked back at Grace.

She walked over to join him, resting her hand on his head as they watched Gabriel ride away.

When he was gone, she said quietly, "But I do want you here."

Tears welled in her eyes and she sniffed them back, rubbing the moisture off on her shoulder.

"Have I made a mistake, Lord?" she whispered, just the question making her chest constrict in pain. "I don't know what I'm doing here."

It was true she'd been forced into coming here, but deep down she'd held out a hope that it was God's will and she would find happiness with Gabriel. But now she didn't know what to do. How could she keep quiet about the tobacco? It disgusted her, and she was genuinely afraid it would make Gabriel ill.

Except now he wouldn't speak to her and she felt more alone than ever. Maybe she should just go home, where she belonged. She could move in with her aunt and spend the rest of her days taking care of her and living out her own life in spinsterhood.

Could that really be any worse than this?

~ ~ ~

Gabriel picked the final tiny golden nugget from the glaze of dark sand at the bottom of the pan, placed it in the jar, and held it up to inspect his haul so far. Not the best day's take he'd ever had, but not the worst either. That was nothing, and it had happened more often than he liked.

He could always use more though. He was barely finding the quarter ounce he needed as a minimum each week, and with the three days he'd taken off for Grace's arrival and the extra mouth to feed, he was behind. But try as he might, he couldn't find the drive he usually had when he was at his claim.

It could have been that Brutus wasn't with him. True, the dog didn't do much other than sleep and, on occasion, make a leisurely patrol of the area, but he still provided some company, and something to talk to when Gabriel was feeling particularly lonely. He'd tried talking to Jed, who was munching on the scrubby grass that grew along the river, but it wasn't the same.

But if he was honest with himself, Gabriel knew the real reason he was so down was Grace. As usual, he'd reacted before thinking things through and he'd behaved badly. It was a habit he didn't seem to be able to shake.

When he really thought about it, and he'd had plenty of time to do that today, he understood that her motives for asking him to stop using tobacco weren't unreasonable. Would he want to kiss a woman whose breath smelled bad? And his standards were no doubt far, far lower than a lady like her. Why she was even with him was a mystery. There was no doubt in his mind that he wasn't good enough for her.

But more than that, she worried that he might get sick. Whether or not she was right about that was debatable, but she thought she was, and she wanted to protect him from that. That meant she cared about him, didn't it?

He pulled his tobacco pouch from his pocket and stared at it. He hadn't had any since the night before, just to see if he could do it, and already he felt out of sorts. More than once he'd had it out and a pinch almost to his mouth before he'd even realized what he was doing. The need for it was intensifying and if it hadn't been for the spruce gum Grace had bought him, he might have succumbed. He couldn't imagine lasting another day without it, let alone however long it would take for the cravings to subside. Could he really stop altogether?

But if it meant he got to keep Grace as his wife, could he really not?

Sighing, he pushed the pouch back into his pocket. He'd got this far. He would try a little longer. For her.

He looked out over the clear mountain stream to the rugged gray slopes on the far side of the valley. It was pretty here, in a desolate sort of way. He'd always liked the solitude of being so far away from other people, with no sound but the water tumbling over the rocks and the wind and the occasional cry of an eagle or vulture soaring overhead. The memories of blood and death faded here.

But for the first time, he wanted to be elsewhere, with someone. He wanted to be with Grace.

Making his decision, he rinsed out the sand left in the pan into the stream and picked up the rocker box to take back to the cabin he used for shelter. He wouldn't stay tonight, as he'd intended when he was angry and not thinking straight.

His wife needed him at home. And truthfully, he needed to be there with her.

~ ~ ~

Pushing aside all worries of her impending night alone, Grace threw herself into her work.

She began with laundry, gathering a few of her items of clothing for washing and then going through all of Gabriel's, using her nose to tell her which needed attention. It wasn't as many as she'd anticipated, but it was more than she would have liked. Not that she was surprised. In her experience with her own father after her mother passed, men left to their own devices tended to be somewhat less than fastidious about how often their clothing got washed.

The laundry took up most of the morning so she made lunch when she was done, took a chair out onto the porch, and ate with the clean clothing wafting in the breeze on the clothes line to her left and the stunning vista of the valley on her right.

When she had rested and eaten, she swept and dusted the house, tidied up, checked on the animals, and planned supper. With all that done, she had to face the fact that she couldn't put off the barn where Fred, Jed, and Goat slept any longer.

Back at home, the only place Grace had never cleaned was the stables. In spite of having staff, she believed taking some of the chores on herself was something all those fortunate enough to be able to employ others to work for them should do. But the stable was where she'd always drawn the line. It was just... revolting.

But there was no one else to do it here, and this was her home now. So she wrapped a scarf around her nose and mouth, pulled on a pair of leather gloves, asked Brutus to wish her luck, and went in.

Ten seconds later she ran out again with a shriek. It wasn't an unreasonable reaction, she told herself as she stared at the open door and waited for her heart to stop hammering in her throat. The rat she'd seen was so huge it could have passed for a small dog.

Pulling the scarf from her face, she called Brutus. He plodded over to her from where he'd been sniffing at the drying laundry.

She stroked his back and pointed at the barn. "Go in there and frighten out the rats, there's a good boy."

He wagged his tail and didn't move.

Edging towards the barn door, she patted her thigh for him to follow. "In you go. Good boy."

He looked up at her, wagged his tail again, and sat down.

She sighed and ruffled his furry head. She didn't want to go back in there while the long-tailed monsters held sway, but without any motivation it seemed Brutus wouldn't go in without her.

And then she had an idea.

Five minutes later she was back with a handful of dried beef, and a very happy Brutus bounding in and out of the barn as she tossed pieces in for him to chase. She'd never seen him so animated and she laughed as he barreled around the interior, startling rodents from their hiding places in his quest to find the tasty morsels of meat. He even chased a couple as they made their escape, although not very far, preferring to return to Grace for more food.

When she was certain all the rats must have vacated the barn, she left Brutus happily chewing on the remainder of the beef at the door while she set about cleaning the stalls.

To his credit, Gabriel had actually removed the straw bedding and whatever the horses and goat did overnight, but he hadn't been overly thorough in cleaning the floors and walls.

"I'll be happy once it's done," she muttered to herself over and over as she scrubbed. "I just have to get it done."

After two hours the worst of it was finished and she stripped off her now filthy dress, washed from head to toe, and collapsed onto the bed.

She was woken by a wet nose pushing into her hand. When she opened her eyes, Brutus' head was resting on the edge of the bed and he was staring at her accusingly. Seeing her awake, he whined.

Yawning, she reached for her watch on the bedside table. It read five twenty-seven.

"Sorry, boy," she said, sitting up and stretching. "I'll start supper soon." Then she remembered Gabriel's instruction to feed the animals at five and groaned. "But first

113

I need to feed everything else."

She gave Brutus a raw carrot so he didn't think she was feeding the other animals in preference to him, and headed outside. After filling a bucket with grain from the barrel Gabriel had showed her in the barn, she carried it to the pasture.

She approached the fence with some trepidation. The feeding trough seemed a very long way into the field and she couldn't help wishing it was by the fence where she could just fill it without going in.

It wasn't that she was afraid of Fred. She loved horses. There had been horses kept in her father's stable at the house her entire life and she'd spent many happy hours riding and taking care of them. Horses, she was absolutely fine with.

Goats, on the other hand, were completely alien to her.

Gabriel's statement that Goat would charge anything if she could get away with it scared Grace more than a little. Would being rammed by a goat hurt? Could she be injured? She was fairly sure she wouldn't be able to outrun Goat, if it came down to it.

She sincerely hoped it wouldn't come down to it.

She placed the bucket of grain on the ground as Goat trotted up to the fence. "Good afternoon, Goat."

She looked up at her and bleated.

Grace picked up the bucket and gave it a shake. "I've got your supper here, so when I come in this gate, can we agree that you won't charge at me?"

Goat's eyes fixed on the bucket and she bleated again.

"Well, I could take that as a yes," Grace murmured, unconvinced that it was.

114

Fred wandered over to them, attracted by the bucket. He hooked his face over the fence, stretching his nose towards the food.

Grace moved it out of his reach and rubbed his neck. "At least let me get it to the trough first."

Opening the gate turned out to be harder than expected, with both Goat and Fred crowding the other side in their eagerness to reach the enticing bucket. Grace managed to shoo Fred back, but Goat was less inclined to be moved. Eventually she simply pushed it open a little, slid through the gap, then closed it again behind her, making sure to slide both bolts into place to secure it.

Goat immediately tried to jump up at her to reach the bucket.

Grace scooted backwards, raising her free hand. "Don't you dare!"

Goat froze at her sharp tone.

She stood up straight and pointed at the animal. "If you get so much as a speck of mud on this dress, you are in big trouble."

Goat's eyes flicked between her and the bucket. Grace could have sworn she was weighing up the immediate reward of grabbing at the bucket against the indeterminate consequences of being in big trouble.

"All right, now we understand each other I'm going to put this into the trough and you're going to wait until I have. And there will be no charging at me. Are we in agreement?"

The goat didn't move. Assuming that as a yes, Grace took a cautious step away from the gate. When Goat still didn't move, she straightened her back, held her head up high in a show of confidence she didn't entirely feel, and strode towards the trough.

She half expected to feel a head slam into the back of her legs, so when she glanced back she was surprised to see Goat trotting along after her calmly and showing no sign of getting ready to charge, with Fred following.

Breathing out in relief, Grace picked up her pace.

On reaching the trough, she emptied the bucket into it and stepped back as Goat and Fred plunged their noses into the grain.

"Well, that wasn't so bad."

Smiling to herself, she returned to the gate, walked out, and fastened the bolt at the top.

She could do this. It wasn't so hard.

~ ~ ~

Half an hour later, Grace was in the house finishing her preparations for supper when she heard a mild woof from outside. Brutus rarely barked, even softly, so she figured anything prompting such a reaction warranted checking on.

She walked outside to find him lying in the sun on the porch, as usual, head up and gaze fixed on the open door of the barn.

Shading her eyes with her hand, she strained to see into the gloomy interior. "What is it? Is something in there?"

When he failed to supply any details as to why the barn was of interest, she walked down the porch steps and started across the yard.

It was probably nothing. Just a rat.

116

Just a small, harmless rat.

Her footsteps slowed to a halt. She wasn't sure she was ready to face a rat by herself, even a small, harmless one. But she had to face up to her fears sooner or later. There were rats and that wasn't about to change, so she needed to get used to it. And today was as good a time as any to start.

"It's just a rat," she murmured to herself as she resumed walking. "Nothing to be afraid of. It can't hurt me. It's just..."

Something inside the barn thudded and she stopped, her heart pounding. It took two tries to get her voice to work.

"Brutus, come here, boy," she called softly, patting her leg while keeping her eyes on the barn door. A few seconds later, a furry head nudged her hip. "Good boy. You just stay with me. And whatever is in there, feel free to chase it away. Or eat it."

She resumed her reluctant creep to the barn, her hand on Brutus' head to reassure herself of his presence and steady her nerves.

There's nothing in there to be frightened of, she told herself as she reached the door. *Nothing can hurt me. Although maybe I should have brought the gun...*

A bleat interrupted her thoughts. From inside the barn.

"*Goat?*"

It took a few moments for her eyes to adjust from the sunshine to the gloom inside, but when they did, her fear was instantly replaced by horror.

"Goat! How in the world did you get in here? And what are you *doing*?"

The offending nanny goat was standing in the barn beside a barrel lying on its side, happily munching on the

117

grain spilling from it.

Brutus looked up at Grace, tail wagging uncertainly. Probably wondering if he was still expected to carry out her previous instruction to eat whatever was in the barn, given that Goat was part of the extended family.

Recovering from her shock, Grace rushed in, waving her arms. "Get away from that! *Bad* goat!"

If a goat could glare, the look Goat gave her before darting around her to the door would have definitely qualified.

Grace made a grab for her as she hurtled past, only just managing a glancing touch to her back before she was gone.

She rushed after her, coming to an abrupt halt out in the yard when she saw the gate into the field. The lower half was pushed out, a Goat-sized gap between it and the fence post.

The bottom bolt. In her happiness at having made it out of the field in one piece, she'd forgotten to fasten the bottom bolt.

As Goat ran towards the gate, for one blissful moment Grace thought she was simply going to go back in. One very brief blissful moment. The next moment she was watching the goat run past, heading for the trees further up the hill that bounded the stream.

"No!" If she lost Goat, Gabriel would never forgive her.

Picking up her skirts, she sprinted after the animal, frantically calling her name. Unfortunately, Goat was a fast runner, easily outpacing Grace, and after an embarrassingly short amount of time she was forced to stop yelling in favor of breathing. Although she was impressed with herself that she managed to run all the way up the hill without stopping.

Maybe all the fresh air was doing her good.

She reached the shade of the trees and stopped, grasping the bark of the closest tree and leaning forward to gasp in lungfuls of air. A smug bleat from somewhere ahead mocked her.

"Rotten animal," Grace muttered, releasing the tree and resuming her pursuit. "If I catch you, we're eating roast goat for the next few days."

She was only half joking.

She continued through the trees to the stream and came to a halt. Goat was standing at the muddy edge, sucking up the cool water. She raised her head at Grace's approach and backed away a couple of steps, looking ready to take off again. Grace watched her silently, trying to work out a way to get close enough to catch her without frightening her off.

It was then that she realized she had nothing to hold Goat with, even if she did manage to catch her. She could hardly carry her back to the house, even if Goat would let her, which seemed highly unlikely.

But she had to get the goat back.

Squaring her shoulders, she moved forward. First things first – catch the animal. She'd worry about the rest after that.

Goat backed away another few steps and Grace stopped again.

This was ludicrous. She refused to be bested by a goat.

"I realize you and I may not be on the best of terms, but the fact remains that I am the human and you are the animal and that means I'm in charge. And frankly, I don't see what you're complaining about. You've got a nice big field to roam in, two horses to talk to, all the food you could possibly want, and no worries in the world. You should try being me for a change. All but thrown out of your home by your own father, having to travel all the way across the country to marry a man you've never met, ending up cooking and cleaning and taking care of chickens and goats which you have next to no experience with, not sure if your husband even likes you. And for what? So you don't have to marry a man twice your age with hairy ears! Do you have to deal with any of that? No, you do not. So what are you trying to escape for? Hmm? You should be happy to have such a peaceful, calm life."

Goat had stopped backing away, listening to her with interest, and Grace resumed her slow advance as she spoke.

"Now I'm not saying I don't understand the urge to be free and live your own life, but you have to ask yourself, what would that life be like? Gabriel said there are coyotes and wolves around here who would just love to get their teeth into a nice juicy goat. I'm sorry, but it's the truth. I'm not going to lie to you. Life on your own can be downright dangerous. So for both our sakes, just do the sensible thing and let me..."

Finally within lunging distance, Grace sprang forward.

Goat darted to the side, too quick for her to get more than a brief grasp of her neck, and ran past her.

And before Grace knew what was happening, a head slammed into the backs of her knees. She plummeted forward with a cry, landing face first in the mud beside the stream with a splash.

For a few seconds she didn't move, the wet mud seeping through her clothing. Behind her, Goat bleated. Grace could have sworn the rotten thing was laughing.

120

She pushed to her hands and knees, crawled to drier ground, and flopped onto her back, staring up at the canopy above her. And she'd thought this place pretty. She didn't know whether to laugh or cry, although at that moment the latter felt more likely.

A hairy brown face appeared, looking down at her, and bleated. And then she began nibbling at her muddy skirt.

Batting Goat away, beyond caring if she ever went back into the field, Grace sat up. To her surprise, not only did Goat not run away, she lay down beside her and rested her head in Grace's lap.

"I'm beginning to think," Grace said, stroking one hand over her smooth head, "that you are just making fun of me."

Goat's only response was to close her eyes.

Grace sighed and looked around them. "Well, I'm going back to the house to clean up. You can come with me or not."

Dislodging Goat's head from her lap, she struggled to her feet, wincing at her aching legs as she looked down at herself. She was covered, literally head to toe, in mud. For once, she was grateful for the isolation of her home. At least no one would see her.

She walked a few yards upstream to the place where the bank turned from mud to rock and kneeled down to splash water onto her face and hair, rinsing off the worst of the dirt. Then she rose and returned to the path leading back to the house, barely glancing at Goat as she walked past where she still lay. After a few paces, she heard a rustling in the undergrowth behind her. A look back confirmed it was Goat, following her. Rolling her eyes, she faced forward and continued walking.

121

When they got back to the yard, Grace was surprised to see Jed in the field with Fred. Both bolts on the gate were fastened.

Gabriel emerged from the house, his eyes widening when he saw her.

Of course he'd choose this moment to return home. So much for not being seen.

He ran down the porch steps and came to a halt in front of her, his shocked gaze traveling down her muddy dress and back up to her face. He raised a hand towards her, stopping short of touching her.

"What happened? Are you all right?"

"Goat escaped," she said levelly. "Ran to the stream. I tried to catch her. I failed."

His eyes lowered to where Goat, who seemed happy now her point was made, stood calmly at Grace's side.

There were a few seconds of silence.

And then he began to chuckle.

It was so unexpected that Grace simply stared at him, her mouth hanging open as his chuckles turned to outright laughter.

"I'm sorry," he gasped between guffaws, "I'm not laughing at you. It's just, you're covered in mud and Goat's there and..." All further explanation was swallowed in a renewed bout of merriment.

She should have been annoyed at him for laughing at her suffering. Her mouth seemed to disagree with her, however, as the corners, entirely against her will, twitched. She pressed her lips together, but a snuffling giggle escaped through her nose instead. She tried not looking at him, but the sound of his laughter was too infectious.

Within seconds she was laughing along with him, her arms wrapped around herself and her cheeks aching. She couldn't remember the last time she'd laughed so hard. Despite the circumstances, it felt good.

When their laughter finally petered out, she and Gabriel stood staring at each other. He was still smiling and, quite unexpectedly, a thrill shivered through her chest at the sight. He really was quite handsome, underneath the facial hair.

"You'd look good without the beard." It was a moment before she realized she'd said her thoughts out loud. The smile dropped from her face. "I...I mean, um, I just wondered what you'd look like without it. That's all." She fervently hoped she wasn't blushing.

His head tilted a little to one side. "Well, maybe I'll put some thought into shaving it off."

"You will?" It came out before she could think about it.

He pushed his hands into his pockets and smiled again. "I reckon a wife should like how her husband looks."

Now she knew she was blushing. She looked down at Goat in an effort to hide it. "Well, I'd better get her back in the field, if she'll let me."

Amazingly, Goat followed her when she walked to the gate. Even more amazingly, she went in when Grace opened it, with just a little urging.

"You're doing well," Gabriel said, walking up to the fence as she pushed home both bolts and leaning his arms on the top. "I know it has to be hard going from your life before to all this."

Jed hooked his head over the top of the gate and Grace

rubbed his neck. "It's an adjustment, that's for sure." She glanced at Gabriel beside her. "You came home. I didn't think you would."

Breathing out a long sigh, he turned to face her. "I'm sorry I got angry."

The tension she'd been carrying since their argument the day before eased. "I'm sorry I made you feel like I don't want you here. I do want you around, very much. I just don't want you to get sick."

After a moment's hesitation, he reached into his jacket and pulled out the pouch of chewing tobacco he always carried with him. To her shock, he handed it to her.

"I haven't had any since last night. I think you're going to have to hide this though, because I want it so bad I can barely think straight."

"You're giving it up for me?" The leather pouch in her hand blurred behind the tears rising to her eyes. She hadn't expected him to just give up on the spot.

His face fell. "Now don't cry. I don't know what to do when you cry."

She smiled and wiped at her eyes. "I'm just... I'm happy. You've made me very happy."

He stared at her in wonder. "I have?"

Stepping in close, her heart pattering, she reached up and kissed his cheek. "You have." Her smile faded when she saw the mud she'd left on his clean shirt. "Oh, I've made you dirty."

His gaze remained fixed on hers, a smile playing on his lips. "I don't mind."

She knew she was blushing again. "I promise I'll do
124

everything I can to help you."

"I think I'm going to need all the help I can get." His eyes went to the pouch.

She wrapped her hands around it. "I'll go hide this. And supper won't be long. I just have to start it cooking." She looked down at herself. "I'll clean up before we eat too."

"I'll clear up the mess in the barn."

She'd forgotten about Goat's foray into the feed barrel. "I'm so sorry. I didn't even know she'd escaped until Brutus pointed it out. I hope she hasn't eaten too much."

He shrugged one shoulder. "It's only grain. I can get more. It's worth it just to see you covered in mud."

He was teasing her. No man had ever tried to tease her before. She liked it.

She gasped in a breath of mock horror, pressing a hand to her muddy chest. "You, sir, are a cad."

A smile sidled onto his face. "Maybe, but I'm a clean cad." He looked down at the streak of dirt she'd left on his chest when she kissed him. "Well, mostly clean."

Very deliberately, she ran one hand down the front of her dress where the wettest mud still clung to her, stepped up to him, and wiped the dirt down his chest and both arms.

"Not anymore."

His laughter sent warm tingles through her chest and she knew there wouldn't be any more thoughts of leaving.

She was right where she belonged.

CHAPTER 9

Gabriel went back to his claim the next day, but this time he left with a smile on his face after having breakfast with Grace.

Something had changed between them. He wasn't sure what it was, but he felt a lot more optimistic for his marriage. And not just the physical side of it. Important as that still was to him, he was beginning to feel as if there was more to being married than the bed.

Where those feelings had come from, he had no idea, but he didn't hate them. In fact, being with Grace simply for the pleasure of her company had become his favorite way to spend time. He'd never felt that way about a woman before.

On the other hand, his tobacco cravings were becoming increasingly difficult to handle. When he was with Grace, she provided a much needed distraction. When he was alone, all he could think about was chewing. So he threw himself into his work with an energy he hadn't felt since he'd first started looking for gold two years before, when all he'd had was a pan, a vague notion of how to do it, and a determination to somehow make it work.

By the time he headed home that afternoon, he'd found twice the amount of gold than the previous day. That was despite having broken his rocker box after kicking it in a rage

126

and having to patch it up before he could carry on. Grace had warned him that his temper might suffer from quitting. She'd been right.

But just the thought of being around Grace buoyed him for the journey home, and when he arrived in the yard at around six he was tired but in a better mood than he'd been since he left that morning.

His good cheer vanished when a shriek came from the house.

He leaped from Jed's back and sprinted across the yard, fully expecting to find some horrific scene when he plunged through the door.

Grace stood in the center of the room, shaking with fear.

"What is it?" he panted. "Are you hurt? What's wrong?"

In reply, she pointed a trembling finger at the shadowy corner by the bed.

Nervous of what he might find that could have scared her so badly, he crept around the bed and peered into the darkness. At first he couldn't see anything, but then a shape separated itself from the surrounding gloom.

He breathed out in relief. "It's just a spider. It won't hurt you. Those ones aren't poisonous."

Admittedly, it was a pretty large spider, but it wasn't dangerous.

"Th-that's not a spider, that's a monster."

He was about to laugh, but then he saw her face. She truly was afraid, her skin pale and skirts gathered around her as if she was afraid the spider would dart out of hiding and run up them. He didn't understand why women were bothered by things that couldn't hurt them, but seeing her so frightened stirred a feeling of protectiveness he wasn't used to.

"It's all right, you just stay there. I'll deal with it."

She backed away a few steps and nodded.

Feeling just a little pleased with himself for his ability to protect his wife, even if it was just from a harmless spider, he crept slowly up to the offending creature and raised his boot.

"Don't kill it!"

Her sudden cry startled him and he had to grab at the wall to keep from falling over. The spider scuttled back into the corner.

He glanced back at her, confused. "I thought you wanted it gone."

"I-I do. But I don't want it dead just because I'm afraid of it." She bit her lip.

He looked back at the spider. "Then what do you want me to do?"

"Can't you catch it or something? Take it away?"

Catch a spider instead of killing it. Now he'd heard it all. "It would be easier to stomp on it."

"Well, sometimes the easiest thing to do isn't the right thing to do."

He glanced back at her again. Scared as she was, she was standing up straight, defiance in her eyes. She may have been afraid of spiders, but she wasn't afraid to stand up for what she felt was right. Unexpected pride filled him. His wife was strong.

"All right, I won't kill it. But I'm going to need something to catch it with." The spider may not have been dangerous, but it was big enough that a bite would probably hurt.

She went to the cupboard and returned with an empty glass jar, staying as far away from the spider as possible as she stretched forward to hand it to him and then retreating to the center of the room.

He coaxed the arachnid from its corner refuge, slammed the jar down over it as it darted across the floor for freedom, and carefully pushed the lid underneath. With the spider safely contained, he stood and turned the jar over so it slid down to the bottom, legs scrabbling uselessly at the glass.

"What do you want me to do with it?"

"Take it far away, so it won't come back inside." She touched his arm as he walked past her and gave him a shaky smile. "Thank you."

The amount his chest puffed out was far out of proportion to what he'd done, but a grin was still stretching his face as he headed outside.

He put the jar down so he could unsaddle Jed and put him in the pasture, then he carried the spider well away from the homestead and deposited it among some rocks.

"You're a lucky spider, to have found her," he told it as it scuttled away. "Be grateful by not coming back and scaring her again."

He was talking to a spider. It was possible he was losing his mind.

When he got back to the house, he found Grace, a lamp in her hand, gingerly lifting the corner of the blanket on the bed with a stick and peering underneath.

"Did you find another one?"

Her eyes stayed on the blanket. "No, but if that one was

here, there might be more."

Watching her make her way painfully slowly around the bed, he sighed. "Give me the lamp."

It took him half an hour to search every nook and cranny in the entire house. By the end, he'd amassed a jar full of agitated spiders and sore knees from crawling around the floor to catch them, fully aware that a whole new set would probably be in there before he'd even got rid of the ones he'd caught. But the grateful smile Grace gave him as he carried the jar out gave him a warmth in his chest that was worth the largely pointless exercise. It felt good to be needed, especially by his wife.

This was what husbands were meant to do, wasn't it? His own father hadn't been the most loving of men, and most of the time he'd felt like a stranger to Gabriel, but the one thing he had done was provided for and looked after his family. Gabriel figured that was more important than anything else. Removing spiders may have been pointless, but Grace needed him to do it, so he did. He couldn't help feeling proud of himself for that.

He took the spiders further this time, releasing them by a shallow cave where they'd hopefully make their home rather than returning to the house. By the time he got back, supper was almost ready.

He walked into the barn to wash up and change and came to a halt, staring in astonishment.

His makeshift bed with a milking stool to put the lamp on beside it had gone and a metal-framed bed with a mattress stood in its place, complete with pillows, sheets and blankets. One of the bedside tables from the house stood beside it and a washstand had been created from two barrels, a plank of wood, and a large bowl. There was even a mirror hanging from a hook on the wall above it.

Grace walked up beside him. "Do you like it?"

He looked around, taking everything in. "How? Where did the bed come from?"

"I took the buggy into town and asked Pastor and Mrs. Jones if they knew of anyone who might have a bed I could borrow for a few days. Turned out they had one that was perfect. It screws together so it was easy to take apart and we managed to get it into the buggy with the mattress rolled up. Then I brought it home and put it back together."

"By yourself?"

She laughed. "Of course by myself. I'm a woman, I'm not helpless."

"I didn't mean..."

"I know." She was smiling. "So do you like it?"

He sat on the bed, a real bed, and grinned. "This is real nice, thank you."

She looked at the floor. "I just want you to know how grateful I am that you're waiting for me. I know it's my fault that you're sleeping out here and I'm sorry, but I promise it won't be forever and..."

He reached out to touch her hand. "You don't have to be sorry. No man has the right to make a woman do anything she doesn't want to. I can wait. You take as much time as you need."

Had he just said that?

Her face lit up in a radiant smile. "Thank you." She glanced back at the house, a hint of pink touching her cheeks.

"Well, I should get back to supper. It'll be ready in a few minutes."

"I'll wash up and be right there."

She nodded, still smiling, and headed for the house. When she was out of sight inside, Gabriel flopped onto his back. The mattress bounced beneath him.

Had he really just told her to take as much time as she needed before she let him into her bed?

He had.

And what was even more bewildering, he'd meant it.

What was happening to him?

The teasing aroma of Grace's cooking had his mouth watering as soon as he walked into the house. He joined her at the table and closed his eyes, waiting for her to say the blessing.

"Lord," she said, "thank You for this food and for Your abundant provision. Thank You for keeping us both safe today. And I want to especially thank You for Gabriel, for the way he helped me with the spiders and for his patience and understanding. Thank You for bringing me here. I'm very glad I came. In the Name of the Lord Jesus, Amen."

Her prayer set Gabriel's heart thumping. He opened his eyes to see her cutting two slices of the pie sitting in the center of the table.

"Are you truly glad you're here?" He'd never asked her before, but her answer was suddenly important to him.

She smiled. "I'm very glad I'm here. I don't think many other men would have spent all that time getting the spiders out just because I'm afraid of them. I truly am grateful."

As far as he was concerned, any man who wouldn't do

anything he could to gain Grace's favor was a fool. "You ever need anything, whatever it is, you just ask me."

"I will."

He was glad she was there too. At that moment, he didn't think he'd ever been more glad of anything in his life.

CHAPTER 10

The sound of hoof beats in the yard interrupted Grace while she was sweeping the floor the next morning. She leaned the broom against the table, mystified as to who would be visiting the tiny homestead. No one ever seemed to come here. Maybe Gabriel had returned for some reason.

Brutus scrambled to his feet and followed her to the door, stopping beside her on the porch outside.

"Good morning, Mrs. Silversmith." Mr. Fowler raised his hat in greeting from where he sat on his horse in the middle of the yard.

Grace nodded in return. "Good morning, Mr. Fowler. I'm afraid my husband isn't here right now." It occurred to her that it wasn't wise to admit that to a virtual stranger when she was all alone, so she added, "But he's due back anytime."

"That's all right, ma'am, I didn't come to see him. I came to talk to you." He smiled, looking completely unthreatening.

She fought the urge to glance back into the house where Gabriel's revolver sat on the bookcase. Although Mr. Fowler had given her no cause to suspect him of anything, Gabriel's reaction to him on his first visit had her on alert.

He rose up in the stirrups and Brutus took a few paces

forward to the edge of the porch, emitting a low growl. Grace stared at him in astonishment. She'd never once seen the laid back dog display any threatening behavior at all. It made her even more wary.

Mr. Fowler froze in the process of dismounting and glanced back at the huge dog. "Would you mind putting him inside while we talk? He's making my horse nervous."

His horse? How stupid did he think she was?

"He's fine right here."

His throat bobbed as he rotated himself back into the saddle. "Of course. Nice dog."

Brutus would be getting a treat once the man left.

"So what can I do for you, Mr. Fowler?"

Brutus had stopped growling but was still standing in front of Grace at the top of the porch steps, posture rigid and eyes fixed on the intruder.

Mr. Fowler stared at him for a few moments before moving his gaze back to Grace. "I feared you may have got the wrong impression of me from our first meeting. I would like to correct that."

"Did I?"

His smile appeared somewhat forced. "Your husband's view of me is no doubt colored by his reluctance to sell his claim, and I understand that completely. A man sets out to do something, he wants to see it through to the end. Don't get me wrong, I admire him for that, but I think it's clouding his good judgment."

"Is it?"

"I fear that it is." He glanced at Brutus for a moment. "Mrs. Silversmith, I'm going to be honest with you, I was hoping to enlist your help in changing his mind. I can tell you're an intelligent woman and, as a husband myself, I'm of the opinion that wives often display more sense than their spouses."

She said nothing, not because she didn't agree with him, but because she suspected *he* didn't agree with him.

"Mr. Silversmith's work ethic is admirable, but is he really making enough from his claim to be worth it?" He looked around the little cluster of buildings. When she still didn't reply, he went on. "I can tell you are a woman of refined taste who would rather be living in a civilized town than out here in the middle of nowhere. And with the two thousand dollars I offered your husband for his claim, there would be more than enough money for you to have a very nice house in town."

Two thousand dollars? Gabriel had turned down two *thousand* dollars for his claim? She tried to keep her shock from registering on her face, but Mr. Fowler's barely veiled smirk told her she might not have been successful.

"That's a lot of money," she said. "You must want his claim very much. May I ask why?"

"It's not a secret. My employers have been buying up all the claims in that area. They're planning on reopening the mines. With the current advances in mining techniques, we're hoping to be able to extract the ore that the miners who previously worked them weren't able to."

"But my husband doesn't have a mine on his claim. He takes gold from the soil. I believe it's called placer mining."

"I know, but some of the ore seams run under Mr. Silversmith's land. Legally, we can follow a seam wherever it goes, but we prefer to own the land ourselves, to avoid any future issues. I'm sure you understand. Which is why we're prepared to give such a generous amount for a largely unproductive claim." His smile put her in mind of a snake.

"Well, thank you for coming by," she said. "I'll give our conversation some thought. Although obviously the decision is my husband's, not mine."

"True enough, but I'm sure Mr. Silversmith values your opinion. As would I, if I was in his position."

She resisted the urge to roll her eyes. His compliments were becoming ridiculous, given he knew absolutely nothing about her.

He tipped his hat. "It was a pleasure to speak with you, Mrs. Silversmith."

Brutus barked as he turned his horse, as if to say 'good riddance', and moved back to sit at Grace's side.

She rubbed his ear as she watched Mr. Fowler leave. "Good boy, Brutus."

She had no idea what to make of the whole situation, but she and Gabriel were definitely going to have a talk when he got home.

~ ~ ~

"Two *thousand dollars*?!"

Gabriel brought Jed to a halt but didn't dismount. The sight of Grace striding across the yard towards him had him nervous.

"I'm sorry?" He was pleased with himself for the response, serving, as it did, both to indicate his confusion as

137

to what she was talking about and his abject remorse for anything he might have done wrong.

She reached the horse and looked up at him. Brutus plodded up beside her and sat, also gazing up at him. Gabriel had the feeling he was being ganged up on.

"Why didn't you tell me?"

He seemed to be all out of clever responses. "Tell you what?"

"That Mr. Fowler offered you two thousand dollars for your claim!"

Oh. That.

He shrugged. "Didn't think it was important, since I wasn't going to take it."

He dropped to the ground, figuring he was in the clear as far as being guilty of wrongdoing was concerned, and draped the rein over the fence

She followed him to Jed's side. Brutus walked around them and touched his nose to the horse's in greeting. Jed snorted in his face and Brutus sneezed and wagged his tail.

"But two thousand dollars! That's a huge amount of money."

"I guess so." He pulled his rifle from the scabbard on the saddle and rested it up against the fence.

Grace followed him again. "Well then, why?"

"Why what?"

When he moved to go back around to remove the saddle, she pushed her palm into his chest to stop him. "Will you talk to me?"

"I am talking to you." He'd never noticed how pretty she was when she was annoyed, with her eyes flashing and just the tiniest hint of pink coloring her cheeks. It was going to make arguing with her so much more pleasant.

"You're not. You're...you're..." She huffed out a breath. "Why are you turning down two thousand dollars for your claim? How long would it take you to make that much from working it?"

Pretty as she was, he didn't particularly want to have this conversation. He stepped around her to unfasten Jed's cinch. "That isn't any of your concern. You don't have to worry about money. I'll make enough to provide for you and any young 'uns we have."

"Gabriel Silversmith!"

He froze, wincing. That was a tone that took him back to his childhood, specifically the parts of it when his mother had discovered one of his transgressions.

Grace marched up to him and planted her hands on her hips. "I ran my father's household, including the finances, for seven years. I set budgets and paid the bills and the servants' wages and the taxes and I knew every penny that came in or left his bank account. Most of the reason my father has any money at all is because I made sure he did. So don't you ever, ever tell me our money isn't my concern."

"I didn't mean..."

Except, he did mean. In his world, men dealt with the money. They provided it and they decided how it was spent. He'd never even considered otherwise. So where did the fact that she'd apparently had far more experience with finances than he ever had leave him?

"I just meant that I have my reasons for turning down Fowler's offer."

139

He lifted the saddle from Jed's back and tried to walk around her. She moved to block his path.

"And those reasons are?"

Why did he always have to explain himself to her? "Private," he snapped, a little more harshly than he'd intended. "So you're just going to have to accept that I have them and leave it at that."

When she didn't answer, or even move, he walked around her and placed the saddle onto the fence. When he'd checked Jed's hooves, removed his bridle, and turned him out in the pasture with Fred and Goat and she still hadn't moved, he began to get nervous. He darted glances at her as he put away his rig, but she was staring out at the valley and paying him no attention at all. At least, that he could tell. But knowing Grace as he did, he suspected that was a ruse.

Sure enough, as soon as he was done she said, "Are you finished?"

Her voice startled him, it having been a good fifteen minutes since she'd last spoken, or even moved.

"I reckon."

"So you'll talk to me now?"

Did he have to? "'Bout what?"

Suddenly stirring into action, she grasped his arm and marched him towards the house. Instinctively knowing pulling away would only make things worse, he offered no resistance.

Once inside, she released him and shoved the door shut with a bang. Then she opened it again, waited for Brutus to amble inside, and closed it once more.

"Why do we have to be in here to talk?" Gabriel said,

shifting his feet.

"Because I don't want anyone to overhear us."

He looked out the window. "There's no one around."

"I might get very loud."

That was it. He wasn't a disobedient child for her to scold. It was time to lay down the law.

He drew himself up to his full height. "Look here, Grace, you just listen to me. You're my wife and I respect you as the weaker sex and all, but a man has a right to his opinions and to decide for himself what he does without being questioned about it. I'm the head of this house and, as such, I don't have to explain everything I do. So you'll just have to get used to the fact that sometimes I know what's best and I don't need your approval."

She stared at him impassively. "Are you done?"

He swallowed. "I reckon."

"Good. Now you can listen to me." She prodded his chest with her finger. "You may be used to women who allow their men to dictate their lives and make all the decisions without consulting them or even telling them why, but if that's the kind of woman you want, I'm not her. I will not sit quietly by while you decide everything without so much as an explanation. And if I agree with you, I will stand with you and give you all my support. But if I disagree, we are going to at least talk about it like civilized human beings. My opinion matters to me and it should matter to you. If it doesn't, you need to tell me right now because we are going to have a lot of problems."

Evidently, the law he'd laid down hadn't stayed down. Not that he was entirely surprised. She was the most

141

frustrating, infuriating, opinionated woman he'd ever met. She was also the most extraordinary woman he'd ever met, and she was right, her opinion did matter to him.

But admitting his reasons for not accepting Fowler's offer meant revealing things about himself he wasn't comfortable discussing. It meant talking about how he felt, something he'd never been good at.

He walked to the table and sat, resting his arms on the wooden surface and staring at his hands. "It's because that claim is mine." He took a deep breath and let it out slowly. "I've moved around a lot since I left home, and worked for other people all the time. I didn't mind at first, but then the war started and I got conscripted and when it was over I didn't want to have other people forcing me to do what I didn't want to anymore, whether it was killing or working at a job I hated. So I saved up all the money I made after that and finally got enough to buy this mined out claim that probably didn't have a speck of gold left in it. I didn't even have to pay for the house, they just threw it in for free. But I worked real hard on it and I finally found gold. Not a lot, but enough to live on and have a bit extra. Enough to get me a wife and finally settle down. It's the first thing I've ever had that's all mine and I'm not going to let anyone take it away from me. Not for all the money in the world."

It was so quiet when he finished speaking that he could hear his heart beating in his ears. At some point during his little speech his hands had clenched into fists on the table, but he couldn't seem to get them to relax. He didn't dare look up at Grace.

And then the chair opposite him scraped on the floor, he

heard the rustle of a dress, and two soft hands wrapped around his. He raised his gaze to find her sitting across from him, her eyes glittering with unshed tears. As he watched, a single drop of moisture broke free and inched its way down her cheek, leaving a shining trail behind it.

"You don't have to cry for me."

"I can't help it." Another tear followed the first and she sniffed and smiled. "Thank you for telling me. I understand now why you don't want to sell it, and Mr. Fowler can offer all the money he wants until he's blue in the face. We're staying right here."

During his life he'd been wrong about so many things that he'd lost count, but he couldn't remember ever being so wrong as when she first arrived and he'd thought she wasn't the woman for him. She was the best wife he could have asked for, in every way.

Unfurling his hands, he turned them over and wrapped them around hers. For just about the first time since he'd left home at seventeen, he didn't feel alone. It was better than he could have ever imagined. With Grace by his side, he felt as if he could do just about anything.

He wanted to lift her hands to his lips to kiss them. He almost did, but then something occurred to him. "Hold on, how did you know he offered me two thousand dollars?"

"He turned up here earlier today and tried to convince me to persuade you to take his offer."

"He came here when he knew I wouldn't be around?" That wasn't just socially inappropriate, it felt like a veiled threat, a message that Gabriel couldn't be with Grace all the time and that Fowler could get to her whenever he wanted.

143

Although surely he wouldn't harm her, would he? But something about Fowler had bothered Gabriel right from the start, so he wasn't at all sure that was the case.

"I suppose he wanted to talk to me alone," she said, "when you wouldn't overhear."

He looked down at their hands intertwined on the table top. Maybe it wasn't his place to take every decision for them, but it *was* his place to protect her. If something ever happened to Grace...

"If you're worried about me being alone, don't be," she said, guessing his thoughts with uncanny accuracy. "Mr. Fowler didn't even get off his horse. He tried, but Brutus growled at him. It was really quite funny how scared he was."

He glanced over at the dog sprawled on his rug by the warm stove. "Good boy, Brutus."

Brutus opened his eyes, thumped his tail on the floor once, and closed them again.

"Truth is, I don't know why Fowler is offering that much. There's not nearly enough coming from the claim for it to be worth it." Since he was being honest, he might as well go all the way. "I've heard that the people he works for have been buying up the claims around mine."

"He told me that. He said mining techniques have advanced enough that they could get more gold from the mines now."

"It's possible, but that area's pretty mined out. It's the reason I got my claim so cheap. There's still gold, but not enough to interest any of the big companies anymore. Reopening the mines wouldn't be worth the money it would
144

cost."

"So you think he's lying?"

He wasn't inclined to believe anything Fowler said. "I think it's a good bet he is."

"So then why would he offer all that money?"

He shrugged. "Beats me."

"Well, I suppose it doesn't really matter, since we won't be taking his money." She looked down at their hands. Neither of them had pulled away. "I, um... I should check on supper. I don't want it to burn." To his disappointment, she slipped her hands from his and stood.

"Grace?"

"Yes?"

He wanted to tell her how much she'd come to mean to him, but an unaccustomed shyness came over him. It wasn't a feeling he was used to, and all he managed was, "Thank you."

She smiled, nodded, and turned to the stove.

An invigorating lightness blossomed in his chest. Maybe being honest about his feelings wasn't such a bad thing after all.

~ ~ ~

Following supper, Gabriel brought a bench from the barn and set it on the porch.

It had come with the house and he'd never had much use for it before, but he'd had an idea that Grace might like to have somewhere to sit and look at the view she liked so much, so he'd spent time over the previous couple of days fixing it up. In the future, he was hoping it would be perfect for snuggling. He'd never had the desire to snuggle with a woman before, but snuggling with Grace was something he most definitely wanted to do.

He took a blanket and two pillows out to the bench and arranged them in a way that could be conducive to sitting close, if the opportunity arose. Then he called her out from the house.

She appeared in the doorway. "Yes... oh!" Her eyes fell on the bench.

"Figured you'd like somewhere to sit out here, if you had a mind to."

As he'd hoped, her face lit up. "It's perfect!" She ran her hand over the newly sanded back before sitting and looking up at him with a smile. "Would you join me?"

He sat down so fast he felt lightheaded for a moment. "Don't mind if I do."

Her laughter warmed the cooling evening air. He loved hearing her laugh. It made his insides tingle.

"I think this might be my favorite view in the whole world," she said, gazing out over the valley where shadows were gathering beneath the pink-tinged sky.

His eyes remained firmly on her. "Mine too."

He eyed the gap between them. Would she notice if he moved closer? Would she mind?

She suddenly gasped, tensing.

He looked around quickly. "What is it?" Had Fowler returned?

"Rat. I hate those things."

A brown furry shape scurried across the yard and

disappeared under the porch.

Gabriel took the opportunity to slide closer to her. He wasn't proud of himself, but he wasn't about to let the chance slip by. "It's all right, I won't let it hurt you."

"I'm not afraid it will hurt me."

Despite her words, when another one darted out and headed for the barn, she grabbed his hand. He wrapped his fingers around hers and moved even closer. He didn't want her to be afraid, but at that moment he couldn't help but be grateful to the rats.

"Maybe if we watch them for a while you'll get used to them."

"Maybe." She didn't sound at all convinced.

"Do you want to go back inside?" It was the last thing he wanted to do. There were only two separate chairs inside. No chance for snuggling.

He really needed to buy a settee big enough for two.

She drew in a breath and released it slowly. "No. I want to stay here and look at my view. As long as they don't come up here on the porch, I'll be fine."

He had a brief vision of a rat running onto the porch and her leaping into his lap. Reluctantly, he raised his voice. "Brute!" Ten seconds later, Brutus sauntered from the house. "Stay out here and keep the rats away."

Brutus wagged his tail, wagged it even harder when Grace reached out to stroke his back, then flopped down at the top of the steps and lowered his head to his paws.

To Gabriel's delight, Grace didn't let go of his hand. After a while, she even rested her head against his shoulder.

The bench might have been the best idea he'd ever had.

CHAPTER 11

The following day was Sunday and they took the buggy into the town for the morning service.

Grace enjoyed returning to the Green Hill Creek Emmanuel Church. Even though it had only been six days since she and Gabriel were married, it felt like an age since she'd last been there. So much had happened in that short time.

Pastor Jones' sermon was inspiring and thought-provoking and she took copious notes on what he said so she could study it later. Gabriel repeatedly darted glances at her as she wrote and she wondered if she could persuade him to study the Bible with her. She wasn't sure where he stood with God, but he was at church with her, so that was a good sign. After her mother died, her father had stopped doing even that much.

"Oh look, there's Amy." Grace pushed onto her toes to see her new friend through the crowd as she and Gabriel emerged from the church after the service.

His head whipped round. "Amy? As in Amy Emerson?"

"Yes. I met her on Wednesday when we came into town."

His gaze searched the crowd around them. "Did she,

uh… what did you talk about?"

"Lots of things." She frowned at the nervousness on his face. "What's wrong?"

"Nothing. Nothing at all." He wound his arm around hers and tugged her towards the back of the church where they'd left Fred and the buggy. "We should go."

"But I wanted to talk to her." She looked back at where she'd seen Amy with her husband. "What's the rush?"

"Hmm?" He glanced behind them. "Oh, I have to fetch something on the way home, from Mr. Ellery. I told him we'd be there soon."

She looked back but couldn't see Amy anymore, but she supposed it didn't matter. She was planning to come back into town within the next day or two anyway, to buy some more spruce gum for Gabriel. She'd pay her new friend a visit then.

Mr. Ellery's farm wasn't far out of town. They drove through a mixture of arable fields and sheep pastures before arriving at a cluster of barns. Gabriel stopped the buggy outside the largest and set the brake.

"I'll be right back."

He emerged a few minutes later carrying a lidded basket which he placed behind the seat before climbing back up.

"What's in the basket?" she said as they pulled away, twisting round to look.

"It's a surprise."

The last time someone told her they had a surprise, it was her father announcing he'd met Felicia and they were to be married. Grace wasn't fond of surprises.

"Is it for me?"

149

"Might be."

Despite her dislike of surprises, the way in which he was obviously trying to not smile had her intrigued. "When do I get to see it?"

His reply was interrupted by a noise.

She looked round, searching for the source. When she saw nothing but the closed basket, she leaned down to check under the seat. Nothing there either.

The sound came again, a kind of mewling squeak.

"Your basket is making a noise."

"Is it?" He stared straight ahead, his face impassive. Although his lips did twitch slightly, just once.

She looked back at the basket again. "What's in it?"

"Guess you'd better check."

He didn't need to tell her twice. Now dying to know what his gift was, she set it on her lap and opened the lid a crack. A pair of blue eyes peered at her from the gloomy depths. Gasping in delight, she threw back the lid and was greeted with a squeaky meow.

"Oh!" She reached inside and carefully lifted out a tabby kitten. "He's adorable! Does he have a name? Or is he a she?"

"He's a he and he doesn't have a name. Figured you'd like to name him, seeing as I got him for you."

She placed the basket back behind the seat and cradled the tiny ball of fluff on her lap, gently stroking his soft fur as he looked around with wide eyes.

"What would you call him?"

"I'm not the right person to ask. Only thing I ever named was Goat because I couldn't think of anything else. When we have young 'uns, I'll leave the naming to you."

The thought of having his children sent an unexpected thrill through her chest. Feeling her cheeks heating, she lowered her eyes to the kitten in her lap, hoping Gabriel wouldn't notice.

"John Ellery said his mother's a good mouser," he said. "Reckon once he's grown a bit he'll clear the rats right out."

Understanding dawned. "You got him for me because I'm scared of the rats?"

"Yup."

A rush of affection swept over her, for this man who didn't understand her and possibly thought she was crazy, and yet cared for her anyway. "Thank you. This means so much to me."

He looked at her quizzically. "It's only a kitten."

"But he's my kitten. You got him for me to make me feel better. That means a lot."

"Never thought of it like that. I just don't want you to be afraid anymore."

She smiled. "And that makes it even better."

He looked bemused. "I think you're giving me too much credit."

"I don't think so at all." Her heart pattering, she wound her arm through his, the pattering turning to a leap when he smiled at her. Feeling awkward and thrilled at the same time, she dropped her gaze to the kitten. "I think I will name him... Ratbane."

He let out a bark of laughter. "Ratbane?"

"Because he will be the bane of rats, once he gets bigger. It's poetic."

There was half a minute of silence. Ratbane curled into a

ball on her lap and began to purr.

"I think," Gabriel said slowly, "that I would like to help with naming our children after all. Could we maybe call him R.B.?"

Laughing softly, she rested her head against her husband's shoulder. "I think R.B. is perfect."

As they drove towards home, there was more movement in her Good Things About Being in California and Married to Gabriel list.

1) She loved the animals, even Goat. And now she had a new kitten to love too.

2) Gabriel.

3) The scenery outside the house, with the mountains behind and the valley stretched out in front, was stunning.

4) The town was nice, and she'd made some friends. And even though they lived so far away, she didn't mind so much now.

5) The house was cozy and warm and felt more like home every day.

6) Even if Felicia had been there Grace wouldn't have cared about any of her snide remarks, because Gabriel thought she was fine just as she was.

At this rate, he would soon be at number one. And then what would she do?

~ ~ ~

Brutus sauntered from the barn to meet them when they reached home. His eyes fixed immediately on the kitten in Grace's hand as Gabriel helped her to the ground.

152

She held the little fluffball against her protectively. "Will he be all right with R.B.? Does he like cats?"

"I don't know as he's ever seen one." He rubbed Brutus' head. "No eating the kitten, Brute. He's not a snack."

She gasped in horror. "*Eat* him?"

He chuckled. "I'm just joking."

He was, mostly, although he wasn't entirely sure how Brutus would react to the kitten.

Ratbane. He hadn't seen that coming. He would have expected her to name him something like Fluff or Kitty. Not Ratbane. She continued to surprise him. He liked that.

He also liked how she'd wrapped her arm around his and rested her head against his shoulder for much of the journey home. He'd liked that a lot.

He followed her into the house, Brutus trotting along after them.

She looked at the tiny kitten in her arms then at the massive dog gazing up at him in fascination. "I'm scared."

Gabriel pulled out a chair from beneath the kitchen table and turned it round. "How about you sit here with R.B. on your lap and I'll stand right here beside you so I can pull Brutus away if he tries anything? Although I'm sure he won't."

She released a small sigh and nodded. Brutus followed her to the chair like a magnet, wagging his tail when she sat.

She held the kitten tight against her chest with one hand, reaching out the other to stroke Brutus. "You have to be gentle with him, understand? He's only little."

Brutus wagged his tail harder, his eyes fixed on R.B.

Gabriel braced himself in case he had to pull the huge

dog away, although he wasn't entirely sure he'd be able to if Brutus decided he really wanted to do something. When it came down to it, he was well aware that his dog was stronger than he was.

Her brow furrowed, Grace hesitantly placed the kitten in her lap. R.B. arched his back and hissed at Brutus, impressing Gabriel no end. The little thing was a fighter.

Brutus reached his nose towards the kitten smaller than his head. R.B. hissed again and he jerked back, his tail stilling. Then he stretched forward again.

Gabriel held his breath.

And then Brutus sat down, his tail swishing slowly back and forth across the floor. R.B. watched him for a while and then, having apparently decided it was safe, walked forward on Grace's lap. He touched his tiny nose to Brutus' huge one then rubbed his face around his muzzle.

Grace raised her eyes to Gabriel and smiled in a way that made his heart thump. "I think they like each other."

"Yup."

He couldn't fathom why it should make him so happy to see her happy. Was this what being a husband meant?

He'd thought it was all about having a woman to cook and clean and warm his bed, but he was beginning to understand it was so much more than that. It was friendship and support and conversation and, alien as it was to him, having another person's happiness mean more to him than his own.

All in all, he liked the reality better than his misconceptions.

CHAPTER 12

Grace jolted awake, her heart thumping. The knock on the door that had startled her from sleep sounded again.

Brutus scrambled to his feet, dislodging R.B. who had been curled up between his paws, and trotted to the door. He wagged his tail when he sniffed at the bottom.

She sat up and reached for her robe. "Just a moment."

When she opened the door, Gabriel was outside, one hand gripping the doorframe, his head down and shoulders hunched. The moon cast highlights over his disheveled hair.

Chest heaving as if he'd been running, he raised haggard eyes. "Where is it?"

"Where's what?"

"My tobacco!" She flinched at his raised voice and he closed his eyes. "I'm sorry. I just need my tobacco."

"But you've been doing so well."

He let go of the frame and smacked his hand into the wall beside the door. "I *haven't* been doing well! It's killing me! Just tell me where it is."

She'd seen him angry before, but this was different. There was a desperation about him this time she'd never seen.

"Come in."

She guided him to one of the chairs then lit two lamps, placing one beside him and the other on the table. Then she lit the stove.

"What are you doing?" he said, watching her.

"I'm making what my mama used to make to help my daddy sleep when he was going through the cravings you're feeling."

She poured the milk left over from supper into a saucepan, covered it with a lid, and set it on one of the hot plates. Then she pulled the second chair in close to him and sat.

Brutus lifted his head from where it rested on Gabriel's knee and returned to his rug by the warming stove. R.B. snuggled back into his side.

"Are you going to give me my tobacco?"

"If you truly want me to, yes. But not right away."

His hands fisted in his lap. "You don't want to be with me right now. I don't know if I can hold my temper."

She reached out and wrapped both hands around his. "I trust you."

Even though they'd only known each other for a week, she was absolutely certain he wasn't a violent man. If he had been, she knew he wouldn't still be sleeping in the barn.

He stared at her fingers resting on his. "Maybe you shouldn't."

"I think I should." She raised one hand to his face, touching his cheek. "I'm so proud of you. I know you can do this. I know you're strong enough. You just have to hold on. It'll get better soon. Just a few more days."

He stared into her eyes for a few seconds before

lowering his gaze. "I'm not strong enough. You have too much faith in me."

"Maybe you don't have enough in yourself."

He shook his head, pulling his hands from her grasp. "I can't do it. I need that tobacco."

She studied her husband, silently praying for wisdom. Wishing she could take his suffering on herself, even if just for a little while.

An idea came to her. "Give me half an hour. If you still want the tobacco after that, I'll give it to you."

Rocking forwards, he rested his head in his hands and groaned. "Can't you just give it to me now?"

"No. I'm not letting you give up without a fight."

He raised his head, his eyes flashing with anger. "I *have* been fighting! I've been fighting all day, every day."

"Then let me fight with you."

Flopping back in the chair, he looked up at the ceiling. "Half an hour? You promise?"

"Half an hour." She didn't know how she'd do it, but she had to try.

He released a long breath. "What do you want me to do?"

Relieved, she rose to check on the milk heating on the stove. "First, you drink my mother's famous, in our house at least, warm milk with honey and cinnamon. Then we'll talk. You need to do something, to take your mind off the tobacco."

His chest rose and fell in a sigh. "I don't think that's possible, even for you."

"We'll see."

157

She glanced at him to find him watching her with such intensity it made her breath hitch.

"I'm not sure as there's another woman on earth who could have got my tobacco away from me."

"Is that good or bad?" She said it lightly, as if she was joking, but she held her breath for the answer.

His mouth turned up in a small smile. "Ask me in half an hour."

~ ~ ~

Gabriel woke with a crick in his neck and a stiff back. Still drifting in the hazy fog of sleep, he was confused as to why, until he realized he was sitting in a chair, a blanket tucked over him.

He looked at the bed where Grace was fast asleep, the covers pulled up under her chin and her hair curling around her shoulders, partially covering her face. Memories of the previous night returned, of the desperate need for tobacco that had driven him to the house, and the way she had calmed him, simply by being there.

They'd talked for well over an hour and it had worked. He couldn't remember falling asleep. It must have been her who had put the blanket over him. She'd brought him back from the edge and he was glad of it. Only Grace could have done that.

He found himself smiling, despite his discomfort at having slept in the chair all night. If someone had told him that getting married would require him to give up not only his bed and, to all intents and purposes, his house, but also his tobacco, he'd have abandoned the idea and stayed single for the rest of his life. If they'd then told him he would have been happy anyway, he'd have thought them insane. But he'd have been wrong.

Marrying Grace felt like the best thing he'd ever done. Admittedly, his life thus far hadn't been filled with inspired decisions, but she was the shining exception in a sea of ineptitude.

He rose with a grimace, pressed both hands to his back, and stretched with a yawn.

He quashed an overwhelming urge to go to the bed and brush the hair from her face and kiss her cheek. No telling what she'd do if she was roused from sleep that way. He didn't want to experience another of her punches.

So he leaned down to rub Brutus' back, touched the top of R.B.'s tiny head with a fingertip, and headed outside to start the day.

Still smiling.

CHAPTER 13

Grace took the buggy into town after Gabriel left for his claim.

He seemed better this morning, the cravings having eased somewhat, and there was no more talk of her giving him the pouch of tobacco. She praised God for that. She'd spent a long time praying for him after he'd fallen asleep in the chair.

R.B. had spent the whole night curled contentedly in a ball between Brutus' paws so she felt confident leaving the two of them alone together. She needed the general store for a few items, most importantly, several tins of spruce gum for Gabriel.

She left the buggy and Fred outside Lamb's General Store and walked inside with her basket on her arm.

"Morning, Mrs. Silversmith," Mr. Lamb said, smiling at her from where he was restocking shelves of canned goods to her left. "Anything I can help you with?"

"I think I can manage, thank you."

"Well, I'm here whenever you need me."

She left him filling the shelves and headed further into the store.

She'd found out the previous week that the general store

was much bigger than it looked from the front. Shelves and tables and piles of all kinds of goods filled the space. She'd loved places like this back in New York. You never knew what you might find.

She went to the candy display first, not wanting to forget her whole reason for coming into town, and placed six tins of spruce gum into her basket. After a moment's thought, she added four more. It wouldn't do to run out. Gabriel was practically living on the stuff.

Next she wandered over to a table covered in bolts of fabric. She fingered a plain red cotton. She had plenty of clothing of her own, but she'd noticed that Gabriel's wardrobe was somewhat lacking in variety. With his complexion, the red would look especially good.

At the sound of voices behind her, she looked round to see three women enter the store.

"Good morning, Mrs. Vernon," Mr. Lamb said, "Mrs. Wilson, Mrs. Fielding."

The three ladies returned his greeting.

Grace raised her hand and smiled. She'd met both Mei Wilson and Lucy Fielding already. Mrs. Vernon, however, Grace had yet to encounter.

"Good morning," she said as the three women approached.

"Good morning," Mei said. "Have you met Mrs. Vernon?"

"Not yet." She smiled at the older woman in the fashionable, expensive, slightly too tight lavender dress. "It's a pleasure to meet you, Mrs. Vernon."

Mrs. Vernon stepped forward and held out her hand.

"You must be the new Mrs. Silversmith. So good to finally meet you. I had hoped to speak to you yesterday in church, but by the time I got away you were gone. When your husband is the town's foremost citizen, so many people demand your time."

Standing behind her, Lucy rolled her eyes. Mei, although clearly trying not to smile, nudged her arm with her elbow. It was all Grace could do to keep from laughing.

She took Mrs. Vernon's hand. "I can imagine how much of a burden that must be."

"It is, but one I gladly bear, for the sake of the town." Mrs. Vernon fairly glowed with magnanimity. "I must say, it was good of you to come and marry Mr. Silversmith. Most women wouldn't have, given what happened with his first..."

"Mrs. Vernon," Mei interrupted loudly, "have you seen the new curtain fabric Mr. Lamb has in? It's stunning. Don't you think it would be perfect for your parlor?"

Mrs. Vernon glanced at her and frowned. "I'll take a look in a moment." She turned back to Grace. "Anyway, where was I? Oh yes, Mr. Silversmith's first wife. So shocking what happened with her."

Grace's stomach plunged to her feet. First wife?

Mei gave her a look of sympathy and mouthed, "Sorry."

"Uh, yes," Grace said to Mrs. Vernon, forcing a smile.

Gabriel had married someone before her? Why hadn't he told her?

"It's so very understanding of you to overlook the whole episode," Mrs. Vernon went on.

"Well, I believe everyone deserves a second chance, don't you?" Grace's mind was spinning. Who was this other

162

woman? Was she still in Green Hill Creek? What had happened to her?

"Of course," Mrs. Vernon said. "You're so right. We must forgive, as it says in the good Book."

She nodded vaguely. "Yes. Um, would you excuse me? I have so much to do in town before I return home."

"Yes, yes, of course." Mrs. Vernon smiled as if she hadn't just sent Grace's whole world into a spin. "It was lovely to meet you."

"You too."

As Mrs. Vernon turned away to look at the curtain fabric Mei was drawing to her attention, Lucy grabbed Grace's arm and led her away.

"You didn't know, did you?" she said in a low voice when they were out of earshot of the other two women.

Grace shook her head. She felt like such a fool, but there was no point in lying. She liked Lucy. "Who was she?"

"Her name's Josephine Carter, although she's Mrs. Josephine Parsons now."

Parsons. "As in George Parsons, who owns the livery?"

"She's married to his son."

So Amy must have known. Of course she knew. Everyone knew. No wonder Gabriel had gone into a panic when he'd learned they'd met.

"Do Mr. and Mrs. Parsons live in town?"

Lucy nodded.

Grace took a deep breath. Part of her wanted to remain in ignorance, but she had to know what had happened, even though the prospect frightened her.

"Where?"

163

~ ~ ~

The instructions Lucy provided took Grace to a small house some way from Green Hill Creek's main street. She walked up to the door, raised a hand to knock, then lowered it.

What if she learned something terrible about Gabriel? What if this woman still felt something for him? What if he still felt something for her?

Sighing, she raised her hand again, knocking before what little courage she had left deserted her completely.

The moment the door opened, her heart sank.

"Good afternoon," the woman at the door said. "May I help you?"

"Are you Mrs. Josephine Parsons?" she said, hoping against hope that the beautiful, slender woman with the shiny light brown hair and sparkling amber eyes wasn't her husband's first wife.

The woman smiled. "I am. And you are...?"

Grace's shoulders slumped. "Mrs. Grace Silversmith."

The smile slid from Mrs. Parsons' face. "Oh."

Why couldn't the first woman Gabriel married have been ugly? How could Grace ever hope to compete with the vision before her? She must have been such a disappointment when he first saw her.

"Would you like to come in?" Mrs. Parsons said.

If she was honest, she wouldn't. She wanted to leave and forget she'd ever seen the erstwhile Mrs. Josephine Silversmith. But she couldn't very well go now. It would be rude.

"Thank you."

164

She stepped inside and Mrs. Parsons closed the door behind her.

"May I offer you something to drink?"

She swallowed against her suddenly dry mouth. "I'd appreciate a glass of water, thank you, Mrs. Parsons."

"Please, call me Jo. We've both been married to the same man. I think we should at least be on first name terms."

It had a certain strange logic to it.

"You're right. And please call me Grace."

As Jo disappeared through a door at the back of the room, Grace looked around. It was a small but comfortable room, with blue curtains at the window and matching cushions on the settee. A vase of butterfly mariposa lilies sat in the center of a small dining table draped with a lace tablecloth.

Her eyes were drawn to an extraordinary painting hanging on the wall, a red haired man astride a gray horse rearing against a blazing sunset. She'd never seen anything quite so dynamic.

"My husband, Zach," Jo said, walking back into the room. "I painted it for him as a wedding gift."

The portrait oozed vitality and heroism. If that was how she saw her new husband, she surely didn't have any residual feelings for her old one. Did she?

"You're very talented," Grace said. "It's a wonderful painting."

Jo placed two glasses of water and a plate of cookies onto the table and pulled out two chairs. "Thank you for saying so. I know it's a bit unconventional, but he likes it, and that's what matters the most."

165

Grace joined her at the table and took a long drink from her glass, stalling for time. Now she was here, she wasn't sure what to say. She'd really just wanted to see the woman Gabriel had chosen over her. What on earth did you say in such circumstances? She had plenty of questions, but none of them seemed appropriate to ask of someone she didn't know.

"I must admit," Jo said, "I expected to meet you sooner. If our situations were reversed, I'd want to meet my husband's first wife right away. See what the competition was like."

Grace choked on her water. Was she that transparent? "I-I'm not here to... I mean, that's not why..."

Jo gasped, reaching out to touch her arm. "I'm so sorry, I'm just joking! I didn't mean to alarm you."

She wondered if her face was as red as it felt. Maybe she should just be honest, woman to woman. "I'm feeling a bit foolish now. When I learned Gabriel had been married before, I just wanted to see you. I hadn't really thought what I would say."

Jo tilted her head to one side. "You have feelings for him."

"I... yes." Was it unusual to have feelings for the man you were married to?

"That's more than I ever had." She sat back, smiling when Grace's eyebrows rose. "I had reasons for becoming a mail order bride, but none of them had anything to do with him. He was just convenient, or so I thought at the time. We were married for less than three weeks and hardly spent any of that time together. Believe me, even if I wasn't now happily married to a man I'm utterly in love with, you would

166

have nothing to fear from me."

That was unexpected, and something of a relief. But something still bothered Grace. "I admit I'm glad to hear that, but why didn't he tell me about you?"

It was Jo's turn to raise her eyebrows. "He didn't?" She rolled her eyes. "Men. Even the best of them can be woefully dense at times."

Grace covered her mouth as she snorted a laugh. "That's true enough."

"Before you came, he asked me not to tell you we'd been married. He was afraid you'd be angry with him for not choosing you first. I don't think anyone regrets that more than him."

"So..." Grace considered how to politely phrase her next question. "There was never anything between you and Gabriel?"

Jo smiled. "Not a thing. We weren't even intimate."

She breathed out a surreptitious sigh of relief. She wasn't naive, she knew Gabriel wasn't exactly virginal, but at least there hadn't been any emotional attachment. That would have felt worse, somehow.

"The only time we even kissed, I was sick," Jo added. "The smell of that awful chewing tobacco made me vomit."

She winced in sympathy. "It's horrible stuff. I've persuaded him to stop using it, but he's having a hard time with that."

Jo's eyes opened wide with awe. "You actually managed to get it away from him? You're a better woman than me. He clearly thinks a lot of you. He never would have stopped for me."

167

Grace smiled, pleased. "You think so?"

"I know so."

She was glad she'd come. She liked Jo Parsons.

"The first time he tried to kiss me, on the day I arrived, I punched him."

Jo's mouth dropped open, and then she erupted into gales of laughter.

Oh yes, she liked Jo very much indeed.

~ ~ ~

Supper was close to being ready when Gabriel arrived home.

Grace glanced out the window to see him drop to the ground from Jed's back. Ever since she'd left Jo, she'd been wondering what she was going to say to him when he got back. She still didn't know.

Seeing her through the window, he smiled and waved. She waved back, her stomach fluttering. Whether that was from nerves or because he was smiling at her, she didn't know. She adored his smile. It was a little higher on one side than the other and it made his eyes crinkle at the corners. He was so handsome.

She turned from the window, suddenly nervous. What appeal could a woman like her possibly have for him?

Despite Jo's assurances, Grace still couldn't quite believe he hadn't at least been attracted to her. She was beautiful. Grace... wasn't. The thought that he might be wishing he'd stayed married to Jo even while he was married to Grace made her heart hurt.

He came inside ten minutes later by which time she'd

just about convinced herself he couldn't stand the sight of her.

Brutus didn't bother getting up from his rug, but he did lift his head from his paws and his tail thumped against the floor. Curled up on his back, Ratbane opened his eyes a crack, stretched, and went right back to sleep.

Gabriel leaned down to ruffle Brutus' head. "Before you came, he at least stood up to greet me. Now I'm just second best." He glanced at R.B. nestled on Brutus' back. "Or possibly third." He straightened and walked around her to lean against the cupboard beside the stove. "Something smells good."

Second best, was that what she was? Was she even second?

She placed the lid back on the saucepan, resting it against the wooden spoon she'd been using to stir. "Mutton stew. I went into town today to get a few things and I thought it would make a nice change from beef."

He gave her an easy smile. "Having you here with my supper cooking when I get home is one of the best things about being married. Don't know why I didn't get me a wife sooner."

She walked around him to fetch the bread from the breadbox, trying to keep her voice steady. "If you had, then it wouldn't have been me."

There was silence for a while as she sliced the bread, not daring to look at him.

"Then I reckon it's a good thing I waited," he said eventually.

The knife stilled in her hand. "Is it?"

169

"Course it is." He took a step towards her. "Grace, is something wrong?"

She shook her head, forcing herself to resume slicing the bread. "No."

His hand rested gently over hers, halting her movements. "What's wrong? Have I done something?"

For a man who could be astoundingly oblivious sometimes, he was far too observant.

She had to take a breath before speaking, staring down at his hand still on hers. "I met Jo today."

"Oh." His hand slipped away.

She finally looked up at him. "Why didn't you tell me you'd been married before?"

He pushed his hands into his pockets, not meeting her gaze. "I was going to. It just never seemed like the right time."

She placed the knife down and turned to face him. Now it was out, she wanted to know everything. "Were you corresponding with her and me at the same time?"

He nodded, his eyes on his boots.

"So you had the two of us to choose from and you picked her. Or were there more? Was I even your second choice?" She couldn't keep the bitterness from her voice. She should have known no man would choose her if they had other options. Wasn't that how it had always been?

Tears burned suddenly at her eyes and she turned and walked away from him, coming to a stop in the middle of the room and crossing her arms. This wasn't how it was meant to go. She didn't want him to know how upset she was.

A good half minute of silence passed with Grace

determinedly staring out the window and not crying.

Finally, she couldn't stand it any longer.

"Aren't you going to say anything?" she demanded, whirling round to glare at him. Annoyance replaced her hurt when she found him smiling at her. "What on earth are you smiling for?"

His smile grew, much to her irritation. "All this time I figured you for a smart woman, but looks like I was wrong."

Her voice rose. "So help me, if you don't start making sense I'm going to give your supper to Brutus!"

Brutus lifted his head at the sound of either his name or the word 'supper'.

Gabriel rocked back on his heels, his smile still firmly in place. "You're jealous."

"I am not!" She was.

"Then why are you getting so riled up over the ridiculous notion that I might prefer another woman over you?"

"I... I'm not. I just don't like that you kept secret the fact that you'd had another mail order bride before me."

Wait, did he just say ridiculous notion?

He shook his head, still grinning. "Nope. You're jealous. And I thought you were smart enough to know that there's no other woman on this earth that I'd rather have as my wife than you."

It was a few seconds before she noticed that her mouth was hanging open.

His smile faded. "I never had any feelings for Jo. We weren't right for each other. I made the wrong choice. If I'd known you I would have picked you, right from the start."

She closed her mouth, with some effort. "You... you would?"

His smile returned, just a little, and he took a couple of steps towards her. "Yup."

She gazed up at him. "So you don't wish she was still your wife?"

He took another few steps forward. "Nope."

"But... but she's so much prettier than me."

Confusion crossed his face. "Where in the world did you get that idea?"

"I..." She waved a hand vaguely in the direction of the town. "She just is."

He frowned. "Grace Silversmith, hasn't anyone ever told you how pretty you are?"

Her mouth was hanging open again, she knew it. "Uh... no. Well, my mother, but mothers always think their daughters are pretty."

His smile returned as he took two more steps closer, so close now that she had to tilt her head up to look at him.

His voice lowered. "Well, if there's one thing I know about mothers, it's that they're just about always right." His gaze flicked to her lips and her heart stuttered. "Grace, I..." He stopped and raised his head. "Is something burning?"

Her eyes widened. "The stew!"

She rushed around him to the stove, just remembering to grab a cloth rather than grasping the saucepan handle with her bare hand. She moved it to the trivet on the cupboard beside the stove and lifted the lid. Steam billowed out.

"Could you pass the bowl from the table?" She stirred the contents rapidly to stop them sticking to the bottom.

He brought the bowl and took the cloth from her so he could lift the saucepan and pour in the stew. Her skin tingled as his arm brushed against hers.

"Is it all right?" he said, scraping the last of the stew into the bowl.

She glanced up at him beside her, feeling her cheeks heat when he looked down at her and smiled. "I think so."

"Good. Let's eat." He touched the small of her back before picking up the knife to finish slicing the bread.

She carried the bowl of stew to the table, a smile tugging at her lips.

He thought she was pretty. And he liked her better than Jo. It felt good to be someone's first choice for once.

But what felt even better was that she was Gabriel's first choice.

CHAPTER 14

"I'm going into town before I go to my claim," Gabriel said at breakfast the next morning. "You want to come?"

Grace considered if she needed to go again, having only been there the previous day. There was still so much to do at home, with the barns and cleaning and...

She stopped, suddenly realizing what she was doing. She'd have thought nothing of going out two or even more days in a row back in New York. Could it be she was becoming used to the solitude of living so far out of town? Was it possible she was even beginning to enjoy it?

Maybe so, but she wasn't going to turn down the opportunity to visit with some of her new friends. Maybe she'd even go and see Jo again.

"I'd like that."

His smile set off a butterfly in her stomach. "We'll leave after breakfast then."

By the time Grace had finished cleaning up and was ready to leave, Gabriel had the buggy hitched up to Fred and was waiting for her in the yard.

His eyes sauntered over the green dress she'd changed into. "That color looks real pretty on you."

More butterflies. Since the previous day when he'd told

her he thought her pretty, she'd been feeling different around him. Strange. Awkward. Happy. She couldn't work out if she liked it or not, but she was leaning towards the former.

"Thank you."

He smiled and nodded and wrapped his hands around her waist to help her into the buggy. She was beginning to thoroughly enjoy getting in and out of carriages.

"What the..." He huffed out a breath as she sat. "Not again."

She looked down at him then back at whatever had his attention behind her.

Mr. Fowler was riding into the yard.

He lifted his hat. "Good morning. Isn't it a lovely day?"

Gabriel moved his hand closer to the revolver at his hip. "What do you want, Fowler?"

Mr. Fowler's mouth turned up in a smile that came nowhere near reaching his eyes. "Just paying a friendly visit."

Gabriel walked forward and grasped the rein of Fowler's horse, bringing it to a halt. "I'll thank you to stop paying any visits, friendly or otherwise. Especially when I'm not here."

"Ah, you're referring to my last visit when I spoke to Mrs. Silversmith. My apologies. I hadn't realized she was alone." Mr. Fowler's eyes flicked to Grace. "I do hope I didn't scare you at all, ma'am."

"No, you didn't," she replied. "I do hope Brutus didn't scare you or your horse too badly."

Mr. Fowler's gaze shifted to the porch where Brutus stood at the top of the steps, eyes fixed on him. "Not at all." He was obviously lying. "Well, I won't take up much of your time. I just wanted to see if you'd had a chance to talk with your husband about what we discussed."

She climbed to the ground and walked up beside Gabriel. "Yes, I did. And I stand with my husband. The answer is no."

Although he still smiled, Mr. Fowler's expression turned hard. "Are you sure about that? Two thousand dollars is a lot of money."

"We're sure." She slipped her arm around Gabriel's.

Mr. Fowler's eyes flicked between the two of them. "Well then, I guess there's nothing more to say. Would you kindly release my horse, Mr. Silversmith?"

He let go of the rein and Mr. Fowler dipped his head. "Mr. Silversmith. Mrs. Silversmith."

"Reckon he thought you could change my mind," Gabriel said as they watched him ride away.

She leaned her head against his shoulder. "Reckon he was wrong in assuming I'd want to."

~ ~ ~

"I have something I need to do. Will you be all right on your own for a bit?"

Gabriel tried to keep his voice casual as they passed the first few houses at the edge of Green Hill Creek. Grace would find out soon enough what he'd come into town for, but he didn't want her to suspect just yet.

"Of course," she replied. "Could you leave me at Jo's house? I thought I'd see if she was home. I like her. I think we're going to be great friends."

He stared at her in dismay. There was no scenario in

176

which his current and former wives being friends was a good thing for him. "You are?"

She laughed at his expression. "Don't worry, we won't talk about you *all* the time."

There had to be a way to salvage the situation. "Just remember, I didn't know then how to treat a woman. I'm a far better man now, thanks to you."

Oh, that was good. He'd impressed himself with that one.

She gave him a knowing smile. "You're learning."

He left Grace at Zach and Jo's house. Climbing back into the buggy, he had the strongest urge to drive away before his former wife appeared, but his newfound manners compelled him to remain, at least until the door opened. When it did, Grace said something to Jo he couldn't hear, Jo waved to him, and they both burst into laughter as they walked inside.

He was doomed.

He paid a visit to Peter Johnson at the town's smithy first, and then went on to the barber.

Marco Calderon waved him into a chair. "Morning, Gabriel. Don't see you in here often. Special occasion coming up?"

Gabriel shifted in the chair, trying not to look at himself in the mirror mounted on the wall in front of him. "Just thought I'd try a change, that's all."

Marco draped a cloth over his chest. "Change is good for the soul, as my mother always says, usually when she wants to change something. What can I do for you?"

Gabriel finally looked at his reflection. It would be fine. He could always grow it back.

He waved one hand at his face. "Shave it off."

~ ~ ~

He felt naked. He was fully clothed and yet he felt naked.

Gabriel pulled his hat down lower, dipping his head and running one hand over his unnaturally smooth jaw. It felt completely wrong, and his face was chilly.

He should have just had his beard and moustache trimmed. Surely that would have been enough for Grace. There was nothing wrong with a bit of facial hair. It was manly.

But he'd had Marco take off the whole lot and now his face was as bare as a newborn's. And it felt... naked.

Pushing his hands into his pockets, he stared at the ground and picked up his pace. He needed to get out of town before someone he knew saw him.

He slowed as he reached the buggy where he'd left it outside the hotel. Grace was already there on the seat, her eyes on a book open in her lap. He was suddenly nervous for her to see him, which was ridiculous because he'd shaved for her, because she'd said he'd look good without his beard. If only she'd kept that thought to herself.

Taking a deep breath, he walked up to the buggy. Grace looked up from her book.

And stared.

And stared.

He swallowed, running one hand across his jaw again.

"You had your beard shaved," she said, after what felt like an interminable amount of staring.

178

"Yes." Did she like it? If she didn't, he was never following any of her suggestions again.

Her hand rose as if she wanted to touch him. "You look so handsome."

For a few moments he couldn't think of anything to say. No one had ever called him handsome before, certainly never a woman.

"I... do?"

A hint of pink blossomed on her cheeks and a shy smile touched her lips. "I think I married the most handsome man in the world."

He almost laughed. She couldn't be serious. Could she?

He cleared his throat, pushed his hands into his pockets, pulled them out again. "Well, um, I guess we'd better get going, if you have nothing else you need to do."

"Yes," she said, sounding a little breathless. "I mean no, I have nothing else I need to do."

He nodded, momentarily forgot what he was doing, and finally remembered he would need to get into the buggy in order to be able to go home.

She kept darting glances at him as he started Fred off. Once they were out of the town she moved closer to him and wound her arm around his.

After a few moments, she said, "I like you clean shaven very much."

His heart did a shimmy around his chest. Or it was indigestion. Either way, he didn't hate it.

Maybe he wouldn't grow the beard back just yet.

CHAPTER 15

It was going to happen soon, Gabriel knew it.

Things were going so well between the two of them that Grace would surely allow him back into his bed any day now. He'd been shaving every day and spending extra time on his personal ablutions, so he'd be ready. His wife wasn't the type to accept a less than scrupulously clean man into her bed, he knew that much.

His cravings seemed to be improving too. Ever since the night when Grace had stopped him from giving in, the intense desire for the tobacco had been diminishing. He hoped that meant he was over the worst of it. If it meant he got closer to Grace, it would all be worth it.

He pushed his empty breakfast plate back and leaned back in his chair at the table, sighing in contentment as he watched Grace wiping the stove with a wet cloth. Delicious food and a beautiful wife. Today was going to be a good day, he could feel it.

Perhaps it would even be *the* day.

"I've decided not to go to my claim today," he said, stretching his arms above his head and yawning.

She glanced back at him over her shoulder. "Oh?"

"There are a few things need doing round the place. And

I thought it would be nice to spend the day with you."

Her smile outdid even the bright sunshine coming in through the windows. "I'd like that."

He was a blessed man, no doubt about it.

The pleasant calm was shattered by a small ball of fur hurtling in through the open door and leaping onto one of the upholstered chairs. R.B. spun round on the cushion and stood up on his hind legs, batting the air with his tiny paws as Brutus bounded in after him. Brutus barked and dropped his head to the floor, backside sticking up in the air and tail wagging furiously.

Gabriel hadn't seen his dog as energetic as he was with R.B. since he'd been a puppy. He vaguely wondered if it would be that way for him, when he and Grace had children.

R.B. scampered up the back of the chair then back down onto one of the arms, hanging on with his little claws.

Grace hurried over to them and lifted the kitten, holding him up in front of her face. "Not on the chair. You'll ruin the fabric."

Unperturbed, R.B. batted at a strand of hair that had worked free of her bun.

Smiling, she placed him on the floor. "It's a good thing you're adorable."

Brutus dipped his head to his playmate and R.B. pounced on his nose. Brutus shook him away, sneezed, and raised his face, his body tensing.

Gabriel saw the warning signs immediately. "Grace, I'd get back from him if I were you."

She looked down at the dog. "Why?"

Before he could answer, Brutus shook his head, his ears

and floppy skin pounding back and forth with such force Gabriel imagined he could feel the vibrations through his feet.

And then it happened.

Dog saliva erupted from the shaking dog like a fountain, splattering the floor, the chair, and Grace.

Having finished his shake, Brutus wagged his tail and sat down, panting. R.B. rubbed around his front legs, sat between his paws, and began to lick himself.

Grace stood completely still, her arms held out to either side as if she wanted to disconnect herself from them. "What... just... happened?"

Gabriel pressed his lips together, but a snort of laughter escaped nevertheless. "Tried to warn you."

She looked around the room. "How... how often does he do that?"

"Inside?" He shrugged. "Never really paid much attention. Once a day or so. Reckon you've just not been near him when he has. It's why I feed him outside. He tends to shake after he eats."

"And, and, and, do you clean it up?"

He glanced around the room. "Depends. It's okay once it dries. Doesn't smell or anything."

She gaped at him. "Once it dries? Once it *dries*? You *leave* it to *dry*?"

He could tell she thought that was wrong. He considered asking her why, but decided against it. "Only sometimes."

There were several seconds of silence during which she stared at him as if he'd grown wings. And then she said, very calmly, "Out."

He blinked. "Out?"

"Get out. Leave the house. And take the dog with you."

"Now wait just a minute..."

"I am going to scrub this house from top to bottom. It will no doubt take me some time. You are welcome to help, but if you aren't going to, you need to get out. Now."

Her voice remained calm, frighteningly so in fact. He may not have been an expert in female behavior, but he knew enough to grasp that a tone like that wasn't something you messed with.

He stood and headed for the door. "Come on, Brute."

Brutus looked at him then up at Grace again.

She reached out to gingerly pat his head. "Go on outside now, there's a good boy."

Gabriel called him again and he stood and followed him outside, R.B. trailing after them. He quietly pulled the door shut and was halfway across the yard when a screech came from inside the house that made him flinch. Even Brutus gave a rare bark, looking back at the door.

Gabriel laid a hand on his head. "Best we stay out here. I don't think she wants to see either of us right now." He suspected tonight wasn't going to be the night he was allowed back into his bed either. "Thanks for that, Brute. You're a real help."

Twenty minutes later, the door to the house opened. Gabriel looked up from where he was sitting in the barn doorway, cleaning his rifle, to see a mound of clothing fly out the door and land in a heap on the ground. Grace disappeared back inside for a few seconds then reappeared with more clothing. That was followed by the bedding, the curtains, and the tablecloth.

He put down the rifle and walked over to the mound of clothes and soft furnishings. "Why'd you do that? They're all dirty now."

She stood in the doorway, her hands on her hips. "Doesn't matter. They're all going to be washed anyway."

"You're going to clean the entire house plus all this?" It seemed like a lot of unnecessary work to him.

"No, I'm not." She fixed him with a look that dared him to argue.

It took a moment for him to grasp what she was saying. "Hold on, you're expecting *me* to wash all this?"

"If you ever want to step foot inside this house again, yes."

That was it. He'd reached his limit. "Confound it, woman, it's just spit! Why do you need to get all riled up over spit?"

She stared at him as if he'd suggested she go and roll in horse dung. "Just spit? It's disgusting! You can't seriously be telling me you are happy to sit and sleep and eat your meals in a house full of dog saliva!"

"It's never done me any harm."

"All that proves is that you're a very lucky man."

"Not with wives," he muttered under his breath.

She narrowed her eyes. "I beg your pardon?"

He considered saying it out loud but, annoyed as he was, he wasn't stupid. "I ain't washing all this. I have more important things to do."

He may not have been able to sleep in his house, or

184

currently even go into his house, but he didn't have to obey her orders. He was the man. He was the one in charge.

She opened her mouth and closed it again. There were a good ten seconds when he was certain she didn't even blink as she glared at him. Then she spun around and marched back inside, slamming the door closed with such force he was surprised something didn't break.

He turned and stalked back to the barn, muttering to himself. "Not my fault she's got her dander up over nothing. I'm not spending my whole day washing all that. What's she think I got a wife for? Cleaning the place is her job now, not mine." He sat on the barrel and picked up the rifle. "Washing clothing's woman's work. Especially when she throws it on the ground!"

And the day had started out so well.

He resumed his cleaning, doing his best to ignore the pile of clothes and bedding. Not his problem, that's what it was.

Brutus wandered over to give it a sniff then flopped down on the top.

After a few minutes, the door to the house opened and Grace emerged holding a bucket. She'd changed her dress and her hair was hidden beneath a scarf. She looked at Brutus sprawled on the clothing for a second then went to the water barrel, filled the bucket, and took it back inside. She didn't look at Gabriel once.

He pointedly continued to clean his rifle. When he'd finished, he moved on to his revolver.

A while later she came out again, emptied the bucket and refilled it, and went back inside. The pile of laundry remained in the yard, Brutus snoring on the top.

Gabriel finished cleaning his revolver and stared at the laundry.

Laundry was women's work. He had plenty to do around his home without doing that too.

She was the one who'd thrown it onto the ground. It wasn't his duty to clean up after her just because she didn't like a bit of dog drool.

She was the one overreacting, she should be the one doing all the extra laundry.

Frowning, he turned and headed for the chicken enclosure.

The coop needed cleaning.

~ ~ ~

It was funny, and by funny Grace meant not at all amusing, how Gabriel's tiny house became so much larger when she had to clean the whole thing.

Dog drool! How could he have left dog drool to dry on everything? Her skin crawled at the thought that she'd been sitting and sleeping in it since she'd arrived. She loved Brutus, he was a sweet-natured animal, despite his size. But the drool. What in the world was she going to do about the drool?

She stopped scrubbing at the bed frame and looked around her. It had taken her over an hour just to clean the walls and there was so much left to do. Heaving a sigh, she picked up the bucket of dirty water and carried it to the door. She couldn't live for one more minute in this house without it

186

being clean. Granted, she'd already lived in it for over a week, but that was before she knew.

She opened the door and stepped outside. And stopped.

The pile of clothing and bedding she'd thrown into the yard had gone and the sound of splashing was coming from around the corner of the house. She put down the bucket and followed the watery noise to an astonishing sight.

A little way from the house a large pot of water rested over a low fire, and a few feet from that was the pile of clothing and bedding. Brutus and R.B. were sprawled on the top.

Beside the pile, a metal tub sat on a low table, and over the tub was bent Gabriel, scrubbing a shirt on a washboard. He straightened, wiped the back of one hand over his forehead, then resumed his work. Several items of clothing and one blanket were already hanging from the washing line that stretched from the corner of the house to a post ten feet away.

For a few moments Grace simply stood, watching him in amazement. The truth was, she hadn't expected him to do the laundry. When she'd said he should, it was more because she was annoyed at him for letting Brutus' drool soak into everything than because she thought he actually would. She was fully resigned to having to do it all herself after cleaning the house.

But here he was doing the laundry, not because he thought it was necessary, but because she'd asked him to.

She walked up to him and, after a moment's hesitation, reached out to touch his arm.

He stopped rubbing and turned to look at her. There

were amber flecks in his brown eyes. How had she not noticed that before?

"I didn't think you would do this," she said.

"I didn't intend to, but then I got to thinking and I reckon you'd know better than me about keeping things clean." He glanced at the pile of bedding with Brutus and R.B. snoozing on the top. "Not sure how you're going to stop it happening again though. I'll say it now, I ain't doing this every day."

She smiled at the huge dog. "I'll think of something. And thank you." She indicated the laundry.

He looked at the clothing. "Maybe we should have a cupboard to put our clothes in, instead of just hooks on the walls. They'd stay cleaner that way."

She would have hugged him, if he hadn't been so wet and she hadn't been so dirty.

"I think that is a wonderful idea."

~ ~ ~

It took Grace the whole day to clean the house. Neither Gabriel nor Brutus were allowed inside for the entire time.

He continued to wash the rest of the clothing, bedding, and curtains, finishing the last of it early that evening. Grace was impressed. She'd been half expecting him to give up at some point, but he kept going until it was all done. He even strung up a rope between the two barns to act as a temporary clothesline so it could all dry.

At the end of the day, she brought their meal out to an old table he kept in the barn that he dusted off and set outside where they could see the view across the valley.

"How's it going?" he said when they'd finished eating, nodding towards the house.

"I'm almost done. I thought, since I was cleaning anyway, I might as well do the whole place."

The fact that he wasn't the most fastidious of cleaners hung unspoken in the air between them. He evidently decided leaving it there was the better course of action.

"Any thoughts on how you're going to stop Brutus doing it all again?"

She glanced at the porch where he was stretched out in a patch of evening sunshine. "I've had some ideas. How easy to train is he? I had dogs when I was younger and I taught them, but I'd never even seen a dog like him before I came here."

"He's smart," Gabriel replied, smiling fondly at his dog, "and he learns real quick, as long as there's treats involved. He'll do anything for food."

She leaned her elbow on the table and rested her head on her hand. "When did you get him?"

He sat back in his chair, staring into the distance as if seeing into the past. "Not long after I came here, more than two years ago now. I wanted a dog that would guard the place, what with it being so isolated out here. I met a man in town who was selling puppies and soon as I saw the mother, I knew one of them would be just what I needed." He chuckled, moving his eyes back to Brutus. "When I walked into the barn where they were, all these puppies came running up to me, all excited. All except for one. He was curled up next to his ma, fast asleep. The man said he was the runt of the litter and he wasn't sure he'd ever find anyone to take him. He was such a tiny thing, smaller than all his brothers and sisters, but he had the biggest paws you'd ever seen on something so little. It would have been more sense to take one of the others, since I needed a guard dog, but I couldn't leave him there, not knowing what would happen to him. So I took him. It was hard to believe he'd ever grow as big as his ma, but once he started eating well and running around here, there was no stopping him."

It again struck Grace, as her heart pitter-pattered at watching Gabriel talk with such tenderness about his dog, that this man would be the father of her children. She couldn't imagine finding better.

He returned his gaze to her. "What?"

She suddenly realized she was smiling. "Oh, just, it's nice that you have each other."

"I guess I'd have been a lot lonelier if it wasn't for him. I didn't say it at the time, but I was worried before you came that you wouldn't like dogs or you wouldn't get along with him."

"What would you have done if I hadn't?"

"Bought you a ticket home," he said immediately.

She burst into laughter. Brutus opened one eye, scanned the yard, then closed it again.

"In that case, I'm very glad I like dogs," she said, feeling a little shy at saying it. "And that Brutus likes me."

He grinned. "So am I."

CHAPTER 16

"So when do I get to see what's going on in there?" Gabriel said the next day as they ate breakfast together outside. He nodded towards the house. "Or am I going to be living in the barn for the rest of my life?"

She laughed a little. "It's almost ready. Just a few more things left for me to do. It should be done by the time you get home."

"I should come home early then," he said, smiling.

She seemed to have gotten over the whole drool issue now. He hoped that meant things were back to being good between them.

The way she smiled at him reassured him they were. "I think you should."

He worked extra hard all day so he could finish up early, and he was back by four. As soon as he rode into the yard, Grace came out onto the porch to meet him.

"Is it ready?" he said as he dismounted.

"It's ready." Her smile looked in danger of splitting her face in half and he could swear she was almost bouncing. "I'll help with Jed. I can't wait for you to see it."

Her excitement was infectious and by the time Jed was in the pasture with Fred and Goat, Gabriel was as eager to see the interior of the house as she was to show him.

"I changed a few things around, to make some more room," she said as they climbed the porch steps. "And I cleaned everything. And... well, you'll see."

Brutus trotted up behind them as they reached the door, looking hopeful.

She stroked his head. "I'm sorry, you can't come in yet. But later, I promise."

Gabriel wasn't sure how the dog understood her, but he sat, tail swishing over the wooden boards and tongue hanging from his mouth.

She turned to the door, opened it, and walked in. Gabriel followed, pushing the door closed behind him before Brutus could sneak inside.

"So, what do you think?" She stood in the center of the room, beaming.

His smile faded as he looked around. "You moved everything."

"I did, but it makes so much more sense this way." She spun around, pointing out the changes. "See, with the bed there I could have the chairs here which gave more room for the drawers over here. I couldn't do anything with the stove, but putting the cupboard here meant I could move the table over so I could get the bookcase in here, and the washstand..." Seeing his expression, she stopped. "What's wrong?"

It wasn't his house anymore. She'd moved everything, his belongings, his clothes, his furniture. She'd even painted the doors on the cupboard an impractical blue. One of them had a white flower on it. A *flower*.

192

"It's all different."

She took a step towards him. "Well, yes, but it's better this way."

He frowned at her implication. "There was nothing wrong with it before. I thought you were just going to clean."

The smile dropped from her face. "I didn't mean it was wrong how you had it. I just meant..."

"I know what you meant." His voice rose. "You meant it's not good enough, just like I'm not good enough."

She recoiled as if he'd struck her. "I never said that."

"But you thought it. I know you had a fancy house back in New York with servants and money and everything, and all you've got now is this shack and me, the husband who can't do anything right." He didn't know why he was getting angry. All he knew was that he wasn't enough, and it was her fault.

She stared at him, her eyes glistening. "I... I didn't think... I thought you'd... I didn't mean to..." Pressing her hand to her mouth, she ran past him to the door, pulled it open, and fled outside.

He stared after her, his anger turning to shame. He'd expected her to shout at him, wave a skillet in his face, spell out all the reasons he was wrong. The last thing he'd expected was tears. He'd hurt her.

He ran to the door, but she was nowhere in sight and there was no answer when he called her name. And then he spotted Brutus trotting out of the yard and he knew where she'd gone.

He pulled the door closed, not wanting anything to spoil her hard work any more than he already had, and took off

193

after Brutus. A minute later he reached the stream and came to a halt.

Grace sat on a rock beside the bubbling water, her hands pressed over her face and her shoulders trembling. Seeing her in pain and knowing he was the cause was like a punch to the gut.

Brutus ambled up to the rock, sat in front of her, and rested his head on her lap. She lowered her hands to look down at him and stroked his head.

Gabriel approached slowly, afraid she would run from him again. A few feet away, he came to a halt.

"Grace?"

Brutus lifted his head from her lap, threw him an accusatory look, and lowered to the ground at her feet.

Grace looked up at him, her face wet with tears. "I'm sorry."

"No, I'm an idiot." He dropped to his knees beside her and grasped her hand. Forming it into a fist, he placed it against his cheek. "Punch me. Do it. Right here. Just do it."

He wasn't joking. He'd take all the pain in the world to stop her tears.

She dropped her hand into her lap. "I'm not going to punch you."

"Then shout at me. Scream at me. Curse at me. Push me in the stream. Please, do something."

She gazed at him with shimmering eyes. "You hate what I've done in the house."

"No! I don't, I swear. I was just surprised and I didn't show it very well. I thought it meant you didn't like how it was before." Sitting back on his heels, he ran one hand over

194

his hair. "I'm no good at all this, at being married. It's always been just me, on my own, since I was seventeen. I've never had to think about someone else's feelings before. I keep getting it wrong."

He dropped his gaze before she saw his eyes burning. Fear he'd been holding deep down inside that she would leave him, that somehow he would push her away, bubbled to the surface.

He wanted to beg her to stay, but the words wouldn't come. The thought of Grace leaving wrenched his heart with so much pain he could think he was dying, if he didn't know better. Why was he so stupid? Why didn't he think before he reacted?

"I don't think I'm any good at this either." Her voice was soft, uncertain, and he risked looking up to see her staring at the water. "I ran my father's house. I never had any brothers or sisters to consider. I'm used to doing things my own way. I never thought that you might not want me to change your home." She wiped one hand across her eyes. "The truth is I'm scared."

His chest constricted. "Of me?"

"No. Well maybe a little, but not that you'll hurt me. I'm scared that I'll be a disappointment. I can't be something I'm not, but I'm scared you won't like who I am."

She still wasn't looking at him. He had the strongest urge to wrap his arms around her, not for a kiss or to assuage his own desires, but simply to comfort her. For possibly the first time in his adult life, he wanted to hold a woman for her benefit instead of his. It felt strange and alien, and yet somehow right. Grace's feelings mattered to him, even more than his own.

Could this be love? Was he in love?

Tentatively, he touched the back of her hand where it rested in her lap. "I like who you are a lot."

His heart thudded against his ribs at his admission. Just those few words made him feel uncomfortably vulnerable.

She moved her eyes to her hand, slowly turning it over and wrapping her fingers around his. His breath hitched at the contact.

Then she looked into his eyes and smiled a little. "I like who you are too."

He couldn't have been more surprised if she'd grown wings and flown away. "You do?"

"Very much."

"So... so you won't leave?"

Her smile vanished. "Leave? Why would I leave? You're my husband. I don't want to leave you."

He hadn't realized just how afraid he was until the weight left his shoulders at her words. She wasn't going to leave him.

She was still holding onto his hand. Slowly, he rose up onto his knees and shuffled forward until his thighs touched the rock and their faces were only inches apart. She raised her free hand to touch his face, just softly, as if she was unsure what she was doing was right, but the feather-light touch sent tingles of sensation zinging through his cheek. He placed his hand over hers, turned his head, and pressed a gentle kiss into her palm.

At the sound of her gasp he drew back, worried he'd been too forward, but the look in her eyes wasn't one of fear.

196

Instead, she seemed pleased. Was she pleased? And then the corners of her mouth turned up a little and she leaned forward a little and all his doubts vanished as he closed the distance between them and pressed his lips to hers.

Her body tensed for a moment then softened as she leaned into the kiss with a sigh. It was all he could do to not wrap his arms around her and pull her closer. He had no idea what he was doing around her. All he knew was, despite it being the most chaste kiss he'd experienced in his entire adult life, it was by far the best.

When their lips parted she smiled slightly, her cheeks turning a pretty shade of pink, and looked down. His heart thumped in his chest, his lips tingling from her touch. This was better than all the women he'd bedded just because he could, all the soiled doves who would do anything for a few dollars. This wasn't just physical; he felt this inside. It made him warm and dizzy and so, so happy. He couldn't remember ever feeling such happiness. This had to be love.

Of all the ways his marriage could have gone, he'd never anticipated falling in love. He liked it.

He brought the hand he was still holding to his lips and kissed the back. She raised her gaze and smiled.

"I'm..." He wanted to say something, to tell her how he felt, but the words wouldn't come. It was all so new to him. So instead he said, "I'm real glad you're my wife."

Her smile grew. "I'm glad too."

Just those three words made him want to shout for joy. Love was strange. But good.

Grinning, he stood, her hand still in his. He wondered if there was any practical way he could keep hold of it for the rest of his life.

"Come and show me what you've done in the house, please? I want to see everything."

She rose to her feet. "Are you sure?"

"Very, very sure."

Her smile ignited such a warmth in his chest that he wouldn't have been surprised to see himself glowing.

They started back towards the house, Brutus sauntering after them.

"You can change anything you want," she said. "It can all go back like it was."

"I won't want to change a single thing."

He meant it, with his whole heart. She could do whatever she wanted to his home. *Their* home. All he wanted was this wonderful woman by his side for the rest of his life.

He was pretty sure he'd be able to secure another kiss when they got back there too.

CHAPTER 17

Without his judgment being clouded by his earlier, unthinking reaction to what she'd done in the house, Gabriel had to admit to both himself and Grace that his house was indeed better that way. Although, since he also managed to snag several more kisses as she pointed out all her improvements, he would probably have happily accepted just about anything she did.

After she'd finished showing him around, she loaded her pocket with a few of the cookies she'd baked that morning, took a towel, and headed back to the stream, taking Gabriel, Brutus, and R.B. with her. Well, she took Brutus and R.B. Gabriel just followed. The way he was feeling, he was ready to follow her anywhere. But she slipped her hand into his for the walk, so he was pretty sure she didn't mind.

Once at the stream, he finally asked her the question he'd been wanting the answer to since the previous day. "So what are you going to do?"

She reached up to kiss his cheek, let go of his hand, and indicated Brutus where he was lapping at the cool water of the stream. "I'm going to teach him to not shake in the house."

He caught hold of her hand again as she moved to go

and spun her back to him. "There's one thing needs doing before you get started," he said, drawing her close

She slid her arms around his neck, a smile dancing in her eyes. "Oh? And what's that?"

His answer was to dip his head and capture her lips in a deep kiss, his heart thrilling at the way she melted into him and pushed up onto her toes to get closer. When she finally, disappointingly, pulled away, her cheeks were flushed and her eyes bright. What had he done to deserve a woman like Grace? He couldn't think of a single thing.

When he tried to tug her back to him, she shook her head, smiling, and backed away. "Brutus and I have work to do."

He heaved a sigh. "Sometimes I think you like the dog more than me."

"Oh, I did, at first."

Smiling, he caught hold of her hand and brought it to his lips to kiss the back. He couldn't seem to get enough of the feel of her skin against his lips. "I'll try not to be jealous. Although I admit I was, at first."

Laughing, she walked to the stream where Brutus was nosing around a tuft of grass and cornflowers.

Gabriel got comfortable at the base of an ancient, gnarled oak, stretched his legs out so R.B. could jump onto his lap, and settled in to watch his wife. His beautiful, incredible wife.

She called Brutus over to her and ruffled his head. He wagged his tail, his eyes darting to her pocket where he could no doubt smell the cookies.

"Now I'm going to teach you something important, so I'm going to need you to concentrate. I know you're a very smart dog and I'm sure you'll have no trouble picking this up. And there'll be lots of treats if you do." His eyes followed her hand with interest as she patted her pocket.

She bent to pick up a thick stick from the ground by her feet. "Look Brutus!" Her tone laced with enthusiasm, she waved the stick.

He bounced in excitement, tail wagging furiously, and bounded into the stream when she tossed the stick into the water. He returned with the piece of wood, dropped it at her feet, and shook out his drenched hair.

Gabriel winced, waiting for Grace to cringe in disgust as she was covered in a shower of water. But she simply waited for the shaking to stop, picked up the stick, and threw it again.

He watched, intrigued, as Brutus dashed into the stream again.

This time when he brought the stick back and prepared to shake, Grace made a sharp *uh, uh, uh* sound that startled both him and Gabriel.

Brutus stared up at her in surprise.

She said, "Good boy," and placed the towel she'd brought gently over his back, holding it there.

Brutus regarded her in confusion, but when she didn't move he gave in to the urge to shake and cover her in water again. When he was done, she removed the towel, told him he was a good boy again, and gave him a piece of cookie from her pocket.

The next time he returned from the stream she again distracted him as he was about to shake, this time placing the towel on his neck. The third time, it was on top of his head.

Each time, Brutus shook into the towel, received his bit of cookie, and got the stick thrown for him again.

The eighth time through the routine, something extraordinary happened. He emerged from the stream, dropped the stick, and waited, without Grace making any sound at all. Smiling, she wrapped the towel around his head and he shook. His behavior earned him an extra large piece of cookie and lots of praise.

She did the same thing a few more times until he was waiting every time. Finally, she gave him an entire cookie and walked over to sit beside Gabriel.

Sensing that no more cookies would be forthcoming, Brutus flopped down in the grass and began to gnaw on the stick. R.B. opened his eyes, stretched with a yawn, and jumped down from Gabriel's lap to join him.

Gabriel's eyes strayed to where Grace's soaked dress clung enticingly to her legs. "You're wet."

She straightened her dress out, to his disappointment. "I certainly am, and it's worth every drop of water. Did you see him? He wasn't even trying to shake before I put the towel around him anymore."

"I saw. That was real clever, what you did."

"I'm hoping he'll remember and wait for me to wrap the towel around his head every time he gets the urge to shake in the house, so his drool doesn't go everywhere. I thought I could sew a bed for him too so I can wash it, say, once a week."

A rush of pride came over him. "You're quite a woman."

Smiling, she gazed fondly at Brutus. "I just taught him something new. He's a smart dog."

"You're a smart woman." He leaned his mouth in closer to her ear and whispered, "I would hug you, if you weren't so wet."

She gasped, her hand going to her chest. "Gabriel Silversmith, I never pegged you for a man who would let something like a little water frighten him off."

He stifled his laughter and pulled at her skirt with his forefinger and thumb, releasing it to flop back to her thigh with a soft splat. "That's more than a little water. You're downright soggy."

"*Soggy*?!"

"Yup. Soggy."

"I'll show you soggy." Rising up onto her knees, she pushed him down onto his back in the grass and climbed on top of him, bracing her arms either side of his shoulders.

The water oozed from her soaked dress into his shirt and trousers. He didn't care in the slightest.

She smiled down at him. "Now we're both soggy."

"Are we?" His soul soaring, he wrapped one arm around her waist, ran his knuckles down her cheek, and before he knew what was happening, blurted, "I love you."

She gasped in a breath, her expression as shocked as he felt.

He hadn't meant to say it. It was as if the words had a life of their own. But now they were out there, all he could do was wait for her response to his confession, heart hammering in his chest.

After what seemed like an age but was probably only a few seconds, she whispered, "I... I love you too."

His entire world rocked sideways, as if everything

changed with those four small words. He would never have believed it if someone had told him how he would feel right then. He might even have got angry at the idea that he could belong so completely to another person. But from that moment, the moment she told him she loved him, he knew that the rest of his life would be devoted to her. And he didn't want it any other way.

Pulling her against him, he rolled her onto her back and braced himself above her, gazing into her beautiful blue eyes. She brushed her fingertips across his cheek and into his hair, her eyes going to his mouth.

And he whispered her name as he pressed his lips to hers.

It was a kiss filled with passion and love. A kiss that sealed their destiny together as husband and wife. A kiss like nothing he'd ever experienced before, fiery and profound.

A kiss that was over exactly eight seconds after it began when Gabriel was forcefully levered away from his wife by a large, brown, furry head inserting between them.

Brutus flopped into the grass and rested his head on Grace's stomach, raising his eyes to Gabriel as if daring him to try to move him away.

She dropped her head back on the grass and burst into laughter.

Gabriel sat up and glared at the intruding dog. "You are walking on very thin ice, mutt."

Brutus thumped his tail on the ground and didn't budge an inch. Grace laughed even harder.

He loved to hear her laugh, although it didn't make the situation any less exasperating.

He tapped his finger on Brutus' snout. "Let's get one thing straight, Grace is *my* wife, not yours."

"Actually," she said, "I think he may be not so much jealous as hungry. I still have two cookies left."

Now he knew, he saw that Brutus' nose was pointed in the direction of the pocket with the cookies.

He rolled his eyes. "You interrupted that kiss for cookies? I expected more loyalty from you than that."

She sat up, moving Brutus' head to her lap and rubbing the top. "Don't be too hard on him. My cookies are very hard to resist."

He moved towards her again, his eyes going to her lips. "They're not the only thing hard to resist."

Brutus raised his head and calmly ran his huge tongue up the side of Gabriel's face.

He jerked back, choking and batting him away. "Brutus!"

Grace clapped a hand over her mouth in a useless attempt to hide her mirth.

"Oh, so you think that's funny, do you?" He leaned towards her. "Let's see how funny you think it is when you're kissed by a man covered in dog drool."

She squealed and squirmed away, managing to laugh and look disgusted at the same time. He made a grab for her, but she scrambled to her feet and backed away, still giggling.

He pushed to his feet and advanced on her until she was backed against the tree.

She pressed a finger into his chest, stopping his advance. "Go wash your face first."

He heaved a sigh. "Fine, but you'd better stay right
205

there."

Her smile made his heart flip. "You can count on it."

He rushed to the stream to rinse Brutus' slobber from his cheek. When he returned, she was leaning back against the tree, eyes shining as she watched him.

He slid his arms around her waist. "Now where were we?"

A furry head again pushed between them, this time with a plaintive whine.

Gabriel's shoulders slumped. "Could you just give him the cookies so he leaves us alone?"

She pulled the two cookies from her pocket and Brutus gently plucked them from her hand and walked away to settle down in the grass with his prize.

Gabriel again slipped his arms around his wife, throwing a glance at the dog to make sure he wasn't about to interrupt them again. Thankfully, he was engrossed in his cookies.

Reassured, he tilted his head to Grace's upturned face. "Let's try this again."

CHAPTER 18

Grace was walking on a cloud, that was the only explanation. If she'd looked down and seen that her feet weren't touching the ground, she wouldn't have been surprised.

Her Good Things about Being in California and Married to Gabriel list had undergone a radical overhaul.

1) Gabriel.

2) Gabriel.

3) Gabriel.

4) Gabriel...

She was head over heels in love. Even more astonishing was that Gabriel was in love with her.

It was more than she'd dared to hope for when she traveled across the country to marry a man she didn't know. God had blessed her more than she could have imagined. The way she was feeling, she might even have been moved to thank Felicia if she'd been there. Coming to California was the best thing that had ever happened to her. The luxuries of her childhood home didn't begin to compare with how it felt to be in love.

"I'm definitely getting a settee," Gabriel said, scowling at the chair arms separating them.

"I'd have no objections to that."

They'd pushed the chairs together, but they still couldn't do anything more than hold hands. He'd invited her to sit in his lap, but she'd been slightly afraid she might crush him.

He kissed the back of her hand and sighed. "I guess I'd better go to bed. It's late."

A whole cloud of butterflies exploded in her stomach. If she was going to do what she'd been considering all evening, she'd have to do it now.

He stood and pulled her up with him, drawing her into his arms. "Are you happy? About us, I mean?"

She wound her arms around his neck, pushed onto her toes, and gave him a lingering kiss that would leave him in no doubt as to how happy she was. "I'm very happy. Are you?"

"I've never been happier." He drew her in for another kiss then stepped back. "I'd better go before I forget myself and don't leave at all." He kissed her hand before letting it go. "Goodnight, Grace. Sweet dreams."

"Gabriel?" she said quickly as he headed for the door, before she lost her nerve.

He turned back. "Yes?"

"I... um..." She lowered her gaze to the floor, feeling her cheeks heat.

He walked back to her and touched his finger to her chin. "Is something wrong?"

He cared about her, she could see it in his eyes. He cared about what she wanted and how she felt. He cared about her happiness. What more could she want in a husband?

"I-I just thought that maybe," she paused to swallow, "you didn't have to sleep out in the barn tonight."

He glanced around. "You want me to sleep in here?"

She nodded.

He looked confused. "Are you afraid of something? Did something happen last night?"

She shook her head. Her voice seemed to have failed her.

"But you want me to sleep in here?"

She nodded again.

He started to turn away. "I guess I could push the chairs together and..."

He stopped and looked back at her when she touched his arm.

"I... I don't want you to sleep in a chair." Her face must have been the color of the tomatoes they'd eaten earlier.

He frowned for a few moments and then his eyes went to the bed. "You mean... you want me to sleep in the *bed*?"

"Yes."

"With you?"

"Mm hmm."

"As in, you want us to," he waved his hands in a pattern that didn't seem to mean anything, "do what husbands and wives do? Together?"

She nodded, biting her lip.

For a few seconds he simply stared at her, slack-jawed. And then a grin erupted on his face and he threw his head back and whooped. Not exactly romantic, but that was Gabriel.

And she loved it.

He picked her up and spun in a circle, both of them laughing, before setting her down and stroking his fingertips gently down her cheek. "I reckon I'm just about the luckiest man on earth, to have you as my wife."

She stared up at him in wonder. "You really mean that, don't you?"

"Course I mean it. Why wouldn't I mean it? You're everything a man could want."

She didn't intend to ruin the moment, she truly didn't, but the tears simply wouldn't hold back.

His smile dropped from his face. "Don't start crying now. Please don't start crying. You know I don't know what to do when you start..."

Throwing her arms around him, she pressed her face into his shoulder. "Just hold me."

And he did. He wrapped his arms around her and held her so tight and so completely that she felt like he would never let go.

"I reckon I'm just about the luckiest woman on earth to have you as my husband," she whispered as her tears dried.

He held onto her for a while longer before he kissed her forehead and stepped back.

And then, to her astonishment, he lowered to one knee on the floor. "Will you marry me?"

She blinked, confused. "We're already married."

"I know, but I didn't know then what being married meant. I didn't know what being in love was. Now I do, I want you to say yes. I want you to choose me, not because you have to, but because you want to. So I'm asking you, Grace, will you be my wife?"

It was all she could do to not burst into tears again. "If I had my pick of every man in the world, I would choose you. Yes. From the bottom of my heart, yes."

A smile spread over his face and he rose to his feet. She expected him to kiss her, but instead he went to the chest of drawers and opened the one at the bottom, returning with a small cloth bag.

"I had these made by Peter Johnson, the blacksmith. I picked them up when we went into town on Tuesday. I was going to do something special when I asked you, although I hadn't figured out what yet. But since we're about to, you know," he nodded towards the bed, "I figured I ought to ask you now. I think we weren't really married before. It was legal and everything, but it didn't feel real. You know what I mean?"

She nodded. She knew exactly what he meant.

"But now it feels real, like you're really my wife and I'm really your husband. So I thought we should have something that makes it real." He opened the cloth bag and the contents clinked together as they spilled out into his hand. "The gold came from my claim. Seemed fitting that I found it myself."

Grace covered her mouth, blinking back tears as she stared at the two gold rings in his palm. "Oh, Gabriel."

He took the smaller of the two and held her left hand. "Grace, I promise to love you, and be faithful to you, and take care of you, as long as we live." He slipped the ring onto her finger.

Determinedly not crying, she unfurled his hand and took the other ring. "Gabriel, I promise to love you, and be faithful to you, and look after you, as long as we live."

As she slid the ring onto his finger, her chest filled with so much love she wondered that she could contain it all.

Drawing her close, he kissed her tenderly.

211

Then he grinned. "And now we're properly wed and all, let's get back to your idea."

She squeaked as he scooped her into his arms and then laughed, all her tears forgotten, as he carried her to the bed.

CHAPTER 19

Grace woke the next morning with a smile on her face. She wondered vaguely if it had been there all night while she slept.

Gabriel lay behind her, his arm wrapped around her and his chest pressed against her back, rising and falling with his breathing as he slept. Being so close to him, especially after what they'd done the night before, felt wonderful.

She hadn't been completely ignorant of what would happen. Her mother had told her the practical aspects of it long ago, before either of them had learned how unlikely she was to find a husband. What her mama hadn't told her, however, was how it would make her *feel*.

She'd experienced love last night, she was sure of it. Pure love. She'd had no idea anything could feel like that. And now, lying in her husband's arms, she felt utterly content. This was what marriage was, and she adored it.

She stayed where she was for a while, simply enjoying the moment, before she began to gently slide from his embrace. Perhaps she'd bring breakfast to him in bed.

"And where do you think you're going?" he murmured in her ear, tightening his arm around her.

She giggled. She wasn't sure she'd ever knowingly

giggled in her life, but this was definitely a giggle. "I was going to get us breakfast."

"Nope."

"Nope?"

"Don't need breakfast." He pressed a kiss to the side of her neck, sending delicious tremors done her spine. "Got everything I want right here."

~ ~ ~

When they arose, some time later, Grace's smile was still firmly in place. She suspected it might never leave.

She started on breakfast while Gabriel saw to the animals. When he returned, he caught hold of her hand as she passed him, spun her into his arms, and kissed her until her legs weakened.

"Wish I didn't have to work today," he murmured against her neck, "but I've taken too many days off lately. I need to go up there. I'd rather spend the day with you though."

"I'd rather spend the day with you too." An idea came to her. "I could come with you. That would be all right, wouldn't it?"

He raised his head. "You want to come up to my claim with me?"

"I'd love to. I haven't seen it yet. You could teach me to pan for gold." The more she thought about it, the more appealing the idea became. "May I come?"

He grinned. "I can't think of anything I'd like more."

~ ~ ~

The journey up to Gabriel's claim was more beautiful than Grace could have imagined.

He took the buckboard up past the stream, following a well worn track uphill until they reached a tree-lined river which they followed up into the hills. The trees gradually thinned as the ground became rockier, the river turning into a shallower watercourse that tumbled over granite shelves and created little waterfalls and deeper pools.

Brutus snoozed in the back of the buckboard, the oft traveled route too familiar for him to take notice. R.B. sat on Grace's lap and looked around with wide eyes for the first ten minutes or so, until he got bored and jumped down to curl up beside Brutus. Grace reveled in the beauty of the scenery they passed through for the entire way.

Finally they came to a place where the valley widened and the river calmed and deepened for a while. Jagged peaks surrounded them, stark against the blue sky, but in the valley the gray was broken by stunted trees and scrubby grass, and even flowers that peeked their yellow, blue, white, and pink heads out from cracks in the rock where soil had gathered and given them a chance to root.

Up a little from the stream was a flat area on which stood a rough wooden cabin, its walls bleached and silvered from the sun. Even though it was the only manmade structure around, it blended into the landscape perfectly.

Gabriel brought the buckboard to a halt and set the brake. "This is it. What do you think?"

She drew in a deep breath of the fresh mountain air and

smiled. "It's so beautiful. I had no idea."

He knitted their fingers together and kissed the back of her hand. "You are the perfect woman."

"You're going to make me conceited if you keep saying things like that." Not that she minded at all.

"I'll take that risk."

She waited for him to climb to the ground and come around to her side to help her down. As she'd hoped he would, he drew her in for a kiss before letting go of her waist. Having waited so long to experience such loving intimacy, she was enjoying making up for lost time.

Brutus jumped down from the back of the buckboard and wandered over to the river to take a drink. Grace lifted R.B. out and started towards the cabin.

"You'll need a key," Gabriel said, digging in his pocket.

She looked around. "You lock the door? Who is there to steal anything?"

"There are other claims up here, although they all belong to Fowler's company now. But I never got out of the habit of locking it up." He handed her a small key. "All my tools and equipment for finding gold are in there. If I lost it all, don't know as I could replace it."

She carried R.B. to the cabin, unlocked the sturdy padlock on the door, and stepped inside. She'd been expecting it to be basic, and it was, but it wasn't unpleasant for that. A narrow bed stood in one corner, a lamp sitting on a stool beside it. To the right of the door were a small table and two wooden chairs, the seats and back shiny from years of use. On the opposite wall to the bed an array of tools hung from metal hooks, and several larger items sat on the floor beneath.

R.B. squirmed in her arms and she put him down onto the bed. He explored the blanket and pillow, apparently deemed it acceptable, and sat in the center to lick his paws.

On the wall above the bed hung an incongruous painting of a ship being tossed on a stormy sea, the purple gray skies above it flickering with lightning and the foam-crested waves threatening to overcome the struggling vessel. Grace leaned in to take a closer look. The artist wasn't supremely skilled, but it had a certain rustic charm about it.

"That was there when I bought the claim," Gabriel said from the door. "Thought it was appropriate so I left it there."

He walked over to her and slipped his arms around her from behind.

She entwined her fingers with his at her waist. "Appropriate?"

"The ship fighting the waves and the storm and yet still staying afloat. It was like this place. Took me a lot of time and hard work to get it so I could work it again. The cabin was almost falling down, what tools were here were rusty and broken, even the road leading up here was overgrown and had holes. There was a mudslide over it in one place that I had to dig out before I could get the buckboard through. Sometimes I felt like I'd never be able to make it work. I felt like that ship in the storm. But then I'd look at this painting and think, 'I'm still floating'."

She turned around in his arms so she could see his face. "I wish I'd been here then. I could have helped, somehow."

One side of his mouth rose in a soft smile. "I won't deny, having you with me would have made it feel a lot better. But

I didn't know that back then. It took you to teach me how good having the right woman by my side would be."

She loved it when he said things like that. "Well, I'm here now. So teach me how to pan for gold and I'll help."

He grinned. "Yes, ma'am."

~ ~ ~

Finding gold in the deposits around the river turned out to be both fun and dull, and rewarding and frustrating.

At first, Grace enjoyed learning how to use the metal pan to separate the dirt and sand Gabriel dug from the area around the stream. It was an undoubted skill, being able to swill the water around the pan to remove the lighter material without losing the heavier, darker sand that could contain the gold.

When she finally, after many failed attempts, got it more or less right, she was deeply disappointed to find not even a hint of gold at the bottom of her pan. Gabriel laughed at her pout, gave her a hug, and troweled more dirt into the pan.

She'd been working for close to two hours, her hands becoming progressively chillier from the cold mountain water, when she finally saw a flash of reflected light amongst the black sand coating the base of her pan.

"Gabriel?"

He looked up from where he was working the rocker box a little way away. "Hmm?"

"I think I might have found something."

She didn't move her eyes from the tiny shining dot as he approached, afraid that if she moved, or even blinked, it would vanish. When he crouched beside her, she pointed a trembling finger.

"Is that gold?"

He took a pair of tweezers from his pocket and gently picked the speck from the pan. Then he grinned. "It sure is."

She waited for him to deposit her find in a small glass jar, only when it was safely inside throwing her arms around him with a squeal.

He hugged her back, laughing. "Got the bug now, haven't you?"

She nodded enthusiastically. "I want to find more."

"Now you're getting good with the pan, want to help me with the rocker?"

"Yes!"

~ ~ ~

They took a break at around midday, spreading out a blanket in a shaded spot beneath a low tree and listening to the gentle bubbling of the stream as they ate the boiled egg and ham sandwiches Grace had made for them.

Brutus sprawled in the grass beside them, chewing on strips of dried beef, while R.B. had his own meal of scrambled egg.

Finishing her last bite, Grace folded up the napkin her sandwich had been wrapped in and leaned back against Gabriel's chest. He wrapped his arms around her and she sighed in contentment. She was sure nothing could ever feel as good as being in her husband's arms. His embrace seemed to have been designed just for her, so perfectly did they fit together.

Unbidden, a thought came to her that had been bothering her for several days - how many other women had he held like this? It was ridiculous to even entertain the notion. What did it matter? His love was hers now, and only hers.

And yet the idea kept niggling at her. He was her first and only love. Was she his?

Giving in to the need to know, she broke the comfortable hush. "Can I ask you something?"

"You can ask me anything you want."

She took his left hand and ran her thumb over the gold ring that marked him as hers. "Did you court any other women before me? Apart from Jo, I mean."

"Nope, never did."

"Did you want to?"

There was a long pause during which a mild sense of panic fluttered through her chest.

"There was one girl," he finally admitted, "when I was seventeen. But her family was rich and mine wasn't. She only paid me attention to rile her father, but I was too young and stupid to realize that. It didn't go anywhere."

"Did you love her?"

"Thought I did, but it turns out I didn't know what love was. Not until you."

There was a minute of silence during which she reveled in the feeling of relief. It wouldn't have mattered if he had loved someone before her, but she was very happy that he hadn't. This was new for both of them. She liked that he was learning as much as she was.

"Grace," he said after a while, "you do know that I... that you're not the first woman I've been with, don't you?"

"I know." She sat up and shuffled round to look at him, smiling a little as she remembered the first night after she arrived. "Urges."

"Yeah." His smile turned to a faint frown. "Do you think that was wrong?"

"Do you?"

He shrugged. "The way I figured it, they were offering and I paid, so what was wrong with that? Except..." His frown deepened and his eyes drifted to one side, as if he was trying to work out a puzzle. "My ma would have been disappointed in me, if she knew."

Maybe this was also the time to ask something else she'd been wanting to for a while. "Do you believe in God?"

"I reckon. My ma does. She goes to church and prays. It's important to her." His gaze returned to her. "You think I need God to forgive me for what I've done?"

"I think we all need forgiveness. It's what the Bible says, that Jesus died for our sins so we could be forgiven."

"Even you?"

"Definitely me. I don't always do what I know I should, and I get angry and think bad things of people." She smiled. "Sometimes I even punch them."

He ducked his head, lips pressed together against an obvious smile. "Reckon I deserved it."

"Oh, you certainly deserved it," she said, to his laughter.

His gaze drifted to where R.B., having finished his egg, was now trying to steal Brutus' final strip of beef. Grace waited. She'd come to learn that, even though it sometimes took him a while to come to the right conclusion, he always did.

Eventually, he nodded slowly. "I reckon I'll need time to think on it, what you said." He returned his eyes to her and smiled. "My ma will be so happy when I write her and my pa about you. She'd love you."

"I'd like to meet her and your father one day." She meant it. If nothing else, she felt the need to thank them for their son.

"I'd be real proud for them to meet you."

Brutus stood, tugged the strip of beef from R.B.'s clutches, walked away to a flat area beside the river, and lay down again to eat the rest of his lunch in peace.

R.B. watched him go. If a cat could pout, he managed it.

Gabriel sighed. "I guess we should get back to work. I just need to do one thing first."

"What's that?"

Sitting up, he pulled her close and gave her a kiss that sent warmth right down to her toes.

"Now I'm ready."

CHAPTER 20

Gabriel stared up at the ceiling above him, even though he could barely see it in the dark house.

Grace rested beside him, the rhythm of her breathing slow and steady. She'd been asleep for a while now, but he didn't seem to be able to join her.

He kept thinking about what she'd said about God and how Jesus had died for his sins. He'd heard all that before, of course, but it hadn't truly sunk in, until now. His sins were as big as anyone's. Now he really thought about it, if anyone needed forgiveness, it was him. Maybe it was time he did something about it.

He slid carefully from under the covers and pushed his feet into his boots. Checking that Grace was still sound asleep, he stood, crept to the door, and slipped outside.

The night air was cool but not uncomfortably so and he sat on the bench in silence for a while, elbows resting on his knees as he gazed out over the moonlit valley.

"I suppose You know everything I've done wrong in my life," he said after a while. "I haven't exactly been a good person. I've gotten angry, thrown a few punches. More than a few, if I'm honest. Lain with a lot of women I didn't care about. And in the war... well, You know all the men I killed. I hope they're with You now. I never wanted to..." He stopped, his voice failing, and swallowed. "Well, You know all that. And I reckon there's a lot more I've done besides." He drew in a deep breath and let it out slowly. "I'm sorry. I can't say any more than that, but You know I mean it. I just want to say, I know how much You've blessed me, especially with Grace, and I want to be a better man from now on. I want to follow You, like Grace does. That's all." After a moment's thought, he added, "Amen."

Had he done it right? He didn't feel any different, but he wasn't sure that he was supposed to. He'd done it, and it seemed to him that was what mattered.

He would have stayed outside for longer, but he hadn't brought his coat out and the cold was starting to bite. So he crept back inside, removed his boots, and climbed back into bed.

Grace opened her eyes, blinking sleepily at him. "Are you okay?"

"I'm all right." As he said the words, the full truth of them filled him. He was all right. A depth of peace he hadn't felt in a long time, if ever, filled his heart. "I'm completely all right."

She gave him a bemused smile, snaking one hand from beneath the blankets to touch his face. "Ooh, you're cold."

He took her hand and pressed a kiss to her palm. "You can warm me up, if you're worried."

Laughing softly, she snuggled in closer to him and he wrapped his arms around her.

And, closing his eyes, he silently thanked God for forgiving him.

CHAPTER 21

Gabriel was humming. He didn't remember being a hummer before meeting Grace, but now he found himself doing it more and more, often without even thinking about it. Turned out, when he was happy, he hummed. He would never have suspected that.

He thought over his plans for the day as he rode up to his claim. With a wife, not to mention the prospect of children sometime in their future, he was going to need to increase the amount of gold he was finding.

Since he'd progressed from using only a pan to building his own rocker box, he hadn't really done anything more. He'd become comfortable with the amount of money he was making, not having the need for any more. Now that he did, he was considering increasing the volume of material he could get through daily. That meant a sluice.

He already had a sluice box, although he didn't use it too often because of its tendency to trap less of the gold than he could with a rocker, but he was now planning something bigger and more permanent. If he diverted some of the river, he could build a longer box that would sift more material in a faster time. And with a sluice gate he could control the flow of water, enabling him to minimize the loss of the smaller particles of gold that might otherwise escape. So today he planned on making a start on laying the groundwork for his new sluice.

It would be hard work, but he was extra motivated now. He wanted to add a couple more rooms onto the house and dig a well, with a pump and sink indoors so they wouldn't have to fetch water from the stream anymore. Maybe one day he'd even be able to afford an indoor bathroom. He smiled as he imagined how pleased Grace would be at being able to take a bath every day. He smiled even more at the idea that he could take them with her.

He emerged from the small stand of trees that marked the edge of his claim and his humming came to an abrupt halt, the smile falling from his face.

For at least half a minute he sat unmoving on Jed's back, numb, mind rebelling at the sight before him. Finally, he slid to the ground and walked slowly to the place where his cabin had stood.

He nudged a blackened, charred lump of wood with his foot. It sent up a small puff of ash.

When he'd first bought the claim, the cabin on this spot had been all but collapsing. He'd had to rebuild it from the ground up. It wasn't big or fancy, but it contained everything he needed for his work.

All that was left now were the charred remains of the thick wooden frame and a thick, lumpy layer of ash.

He looked around, searching for some clue as to how the cabin could have burned down. There had been no storm during the night, no lightning that could have struck. What else could it have been?

And then something caught his eye.

He walked upstream, past the remains of the cabin, to where a mangled, broken pile of wood lay at the edge of the water. Bending down, he lifted it from the rocky ground. It was his rocker box. No burning at all marred the twisted remains. Its destruction was intentional, and all too human.

He looked back at the cabin. No accidental fire was responsible for its devastation. This was deliberate. More than two years of work, all his dreams for his future with Grace, gone. And he knew exactly who had done it.

Hurling the shattered box aside, he strode back to where Jed was nibbling at a tuft of weeds and swung into the saddle.

Without looking back, he started down the track for home.

~ ~ ~

Grace pegged up the final damp shirt and ran her eyes along the clothesline. There was something satisfying about seeing laundry flapping gently in the breeze, the evidence of a good morning's work. Not that she'd call it fun, exactly, but it was comforting to see it done.

She stretched her back and picked up the empty laundry basket. A rest was in order. Perhaps a slice of the molasses cake she'd baked the day before, sitting on the bench on the porch with a good book, before she did some more work in the barn.

In the pasture, Fred trotted to the gate, lifting his head and nickering. From beyond the trees bounding the stream, another horse replied. It sounded like Jed.

Grace placed the basket on the porch and took a few anxious steps in that direction. If it was Jed, something must be wrong. She breathed out when he emerged from the trees, Gabriel in the saddle. She'd been worried that he could have fallen and been injured and Jed had returned on his own.

He brought Jed to a halt by the barn and sat motionless, staring across the valley. She approached slowly, her apprehension returning. He wasn't injured that she could see, but something was definitely wrong.

Reaching Jed's side, she reached up to touch her husband's knee. "Gabriel?"

When he lowered his gaze to her she almost took a step back at the sight of his eyes shining with moisture. She'd never seen him cry before. If anyone had told her, she wouldn't have believed he could.

His eyes moved to her hand on his knee and he laid his over it, drawing in a breath that seemed to shudder through his whole body. Then he climbed from Jed's back and, without a word, wound his arms around her and buried his face in her shoulder.

Wrapping her arms around him, she held him tight, tears pricking at her own eyes without any idea what had happened.

"It's all gone," he whispered after a while, his voice trembling.

She stroked one hand over his hair. "What's gone?"

"All of it. The cabin, my tools, everything."

She pulled back to stare at him in shock. "What? How?"

He raised achingly sad eyes to hers. "Burned, mostly, all

228

except for the rocker. That was smashed, as a message. He wanted me to know he'd done it."

"Someone did it on purpose? Why would anyone do such a thing?" Even as she spoke, she knew the answer.

"Fowler." His voice was flat, but she could hear the anger behind it.

As if on cue, the sound of a horse approaching came from behind her. Gabriel looked up and his eyes turned to steel.

She turned, already knowing what she would see.

"Good morning." Mr. Fowler waved to them as he rode into the yard, smiling as if nothing was wrong and he was merely paying them a friendly visit.

On the porch, Brutus stood and padded down the steps.

Eyes fixed on Fowler, Gabriel released her and reached for the rifle in the scabbard on his saddle.

"Gabriel, no."

Ignoring her protestations, he pulled the rifle free and strode towards Fowler, swinging the weapon up to brace against his shoulder.

Fowler raised his hands. "Hey now, don't do anything rash."

"I should have done this a long time ago," Gabriel growled.

Grace ran in front of him, forcing him to stop or walk over her. She put her hand on the rifle's barrel. "Don't, please."

His eyes didn't leave Fowler. "Get out of my way, Grace."

Keeping one hand on the rifle, she reached out her other

229

to cradle his jaw. "Please don't," she pleaded softly. "I need you."

Finally, he looked at her, gazing into her eyes for long seconds before giving a small nod and lowering the rifle.

"Sensible wife you've got there, Silversmith," Fowler said. "You should listen to her."

Grace spun around and marched towards him. Brutus followed her, a low growl rumbling deep in his chest. Fowler's horse took a nervous step back.

"I have something to say to you," she said when she reached him, beckoning him towards her.

He leaned down in his saddle. "Yes?"

Clenching her fist, she slammed it into his face.

He jerked back, his hand flying to his nose. Brutus gave a sharp bark and his horse danced backwards, almost dislodging him from the saddle.

"If you don't leave now, I'll shoot you myself," Grace snapped. "And don't you dare come back!"

He took his hand from his nose and looked at the blood smeared on it. "You should have taken my offer, Silversmith."

With a final glare at Grace, he turned his nervous horse and left.

Brutus barked again then sat, looking pleased with himself.

Gabriel walked up to her. "I didn't think it was possible I could love you more, but looks like I was wrong."

"I made his nose bleed." She may have been a little in shock. She'd never injured anyone before.

"He deserved it. How's your hand?"

She unclenched her right fist, only then noticing the throbbing of her knuckles. "It hurts."

Winding his arms around her, he kissed her forehead. "Come on, let's go inside and I'll get some cold water for it. That'll help."

"I've never made anyone bleed before," she said as they headed for the house.

"Guess I got off easy when you punched me then."

CHAPTER 22

On Grace's insistence, they drove into town to report the destruction of Gabriel's cabin and equipment to the marshal. Gabriel told her he didn't see the point, with there being no evidence, but he went anyway.

Marshal Cade was very sympathetic, but he agreed that there was little he could do. Still, Grace was glad they went. It made her feel they'd at least done *something*.

She hesitantly related what she'd done to Fowler, slightly worried she'd be charged for assault, but all Marshal Cade did was laugh and jokingly offer her a position as one of his deputies. She felt better after that.

By the time they reached home, the wind had picked up and clouds were gathering.

"Storm's coming," Gabriel announced, looking up into the darkening sky as they pulled into the yard.

She hated storms. "Will we be safe?"

He set the brake and jumped down from the buggy. "We'll be just fine. The house may not look like much, but it's solid. It's survived plenty of storms and it'll survive plenty more." He jogged around to help her down. "I'll bring the animals in though, and get the chickens into the barn."

"I can help."

He kissed her nose and smiled. "I figured you would."

It took a while to settle all the animals in the barn, with the chickens being the major cause of the delay. Gabriel explained that they weren't often handled so, even when cornered in the coop, they were extremely unhappy with the prospect of being caught. When they finally got the last one into the barn, she breathed a sigh of relief.

A fat drop of rain landed on her hand and she looked up at the black clouds overhead. Several more landed on her face.

"Better get inside before it..." Gabriel's words were cut off as the heavens opened.

He grasped her hand and they ran for the house, making it inside soaked and laughing. Brutus spared them a drowsy glance from his new bed beside the stove. Curled up next to him, R.B. didn't even open his eyes.

"I'll dry off and get started on supper," Grace said, swiping the rain from her face.

His gaze heating, Gabriel flattened his hands on the door either side of her, effectively preventing her from going anywhere.

He plucked a chicken feather from her hair. "Can't say as I'm real hungry. Are you?"

She slid her hands up his wet chest and smiled. "Can't say as I am."

~ ~ ~

Some time later, they lay together in bed, listening to the rain pounding on the roof, punctuated by frequent rumbles of thunder.

Stretched out on his back, Gabriel ran his eyes over the twisted strands of Grace's hair splayed over his skin where her head rested on his chest.

She was a remarkable woman. Strong, determined, passionate, with a temper that could match his own and emotions that changed so fast it left his head spinning. And she was all his.

He loved her with an intensity he wouldn't have thought possible, even just a week ago. The desire to give her everything overwhelmed him, but he didn't have everything to give. It seemed more impossible now than ever that he would be worthy of her.

"Penny for your thoughts," she said, lifting her head and resting her chin on her hands on his chest.

His smiled. "I was thinking we should have more storms."

She snorted a laugh. At least he could make her laugh, if nothing else.

His smile faded and he moved his gaze to the ceiling, his fingertips drifting slowly up and down her back. "I've been thinking about what to do. I can rebuild the cabin and I've got a bit saved up so I can buy more tools, but..."

He stopped, reluctant to speak his failure out loud, as if saying it would make it even more real and final.

She took his free hand, kissed the back, and tucked it against her shoulder.

His tension eased somewhat. "I'm just thinking, what's to stop them from doing it all over again? The people Fowler works for have money and power. When they want

234

something, how's a man like me going to stop them?" Admitting how powerless he was felt almost physically painful, but he needed her support, and her opinion. Whatever he did would affect her too. "Maybe it's time I accept that I'm beat. I should just take their money and give up. I can get a job somewhere. Two thousand dollars is a lot of money. We could find a nice house and..."

"No!"

He started at her exclamation, blinking at her in surprise.

"You can't give up. They shouldn't be allowed to win."

"But I don't know how to stop them." He ran his fingertips down her cheek. "I want so much to give you everything you want."

"I already have everything I want. That claim is the most important thing in the world to you. It's your freedom." She tapped his chest with her finger to emphasize her point. "They can't take away your freedom. I won't let them."

He couldn't help smiling at her fervor. With her by his side, he could believe he could face down just about anyone. If only it were that simple.

"I didn't think you even wanted to stay here, so far from town." It wasn't an accusation. He simply knew how she felt about his place, how she'd felt from the moment she'd arrived.

Her eyes opened wide. "Whatever gave you that idea?" He raised his eyebrows and she smiled. "All right, I admit it took me a while to get used to it, but I love it now. I love this house and the barns and Fred and Jed and Goat and the chickens, and Brutus and R.B., and the rocks and the stream and the beautiful view and..."

235

"And the rats?" he said, smiling.

"Well, maybe not the rats, but R.B. will chase them away once he gets bigger anyway." She touched her palm to his cheek. "But most of all, I love you. This is your home and that's your claim and they can't take it away from us." She moved up and pressed her lips to his, then she gazed down at him, her hair falling in a curtain around them. "Promise me you won't give up. Just hold on. God will help us. We just need to hold on."

Heart bursting with pride, he slipped his fingers into her hair. "I love you so much."

Her smile made him wonder if the sun had come out, even though the storm still raged overhead. "I love you too."

She kissed him again and he wrapped his arms around her to keep her there, heart beating fast.

A meow by his ear and a small furry head pushing against his cheek interrupted them.

Laughing softly, Grace raised her head to look at R.B. standing on the pillow, and beyond, Brutus' head resting on the edge of the mattress with an accusing stare.

"I think maybe they want to be fed." She reached out to stroke Brutus' head.

R.B. ran his tiny rough tongue over Gabriel's earlobe.

He heaved a sigh. "Can't we just let them starve?"

CHAPTER 23

The following day, with the storm over and the sun shining, Grace accompanied Gabriel to check on his claim, with Brutus and R.B. riding in the back of the buckboard.

The river that ran through his land had grown into a rushing torrent with the extra rain from the storm, and debris had been deposited over the rocky ground where it had overrun its banks during the night.

They stared at the pile of damp, blackened wood that had once been his cabin. Much of the ash had either been washed away or was gathered into dark, soggy clumps, leaving just the stark, charred remains of the heavy frame slumped over the metal remains of his tools and scattered pieces of broken glass from the window.

Grace slipped her hand into his as they stood in silence, tears pricking at her eyes at the sight of his dreams so callously ruined.

Brutus wandered around sniffing at each piece of tangled brush and wood he came to while R.B. chased a cloud of butterflies from a patch of flowers that had somehow escaped the rain and flood.

"I don't know anything about woodworking," Grace said eventually, "but I can help you build another one. I can

237

learn. You just tell me what to do and I'll do it. And if..." She paused, uncertain if he'd take offence at her suggestion. "If you need more money, for wood or tools or anything else, I can ask my father. It's the least he can do."

He squeezed her hand. "I appreciate that, but I'd rather not. Not saying your father shouldn't help you, but anything you get from him should be yours, not mine."

She wrapped her other hand around his arm, resting her head against his shoulder. "Anything I have is yours, and not just because the law says so."

He kissed the top of her head. "Let's get started."

They began by untangling the mess that used to be the cabin, sorting the remains into two piles, one for pieces that could, with work, possibly be reused, and one for the rest that were now useless as building material. Grace had read that ashes could be used to fertilize plants so she was taking any that remained back to use on the vegetable garden she planned to create by the house.

Some of Gabriel's tools hadn't been completely destroyed, with the metal parts having survived the flames, so once the structure was dealt with he set about sorting them and removing the damaged wooden parts. With nothing else to do, Grace wandered upstream along the bank to check if the storm had done any damage to the valley.

As it turned out, the area seemed more or less the same as when she'd been there before. Gabriel had told her that heavy rain wasn't uncommon in the mountains so she supposed the landscape had developed around the periodic turbulent weather. After half a mile or so, however, she came across an area of the slope that must have been undermined by the water and collapsed. The river was much further away now, if still flowing fast, so she picked her way amongst the rock and soil, searching for interesting rocks to take home for her future garden.

A glint of reflected sunlight caught her eye and she leaned down to pick up a stone, brushing off the dirt with her fingers. It was roughly half an inch across, with a whitish, glassy texture. Intrigued, she searched the collapsed dirt more thoroughly and found two more made of the same material, one slightly smaller and another bigger. She carried the three stones to the river's edge, rinsed them off, and held them up to the light. They were some kind of crystal, probably quartz, although she didn't know how to tell. Maybe they were worth something.

She dropped them into her pocket and made her way back to Gabriel.

He was clearing the area where the cabin had burned down with the broom they'd brought when she got back. It was a good sign. Maybe that meant he had decided to rebuild.

"I was just about to come looking for you," he said as she walked up to him. "You were gone for a while."

"I found something." She took the stones from her pocket. "There's a place where a bank has collapsed and I found these in the dirt. Are they quartz?"

He glanced at the stones briefly. "Probably."

"Are they worth anything?"

"Some. It isn't all that valuable, although sometimes quartz seams also have gold in them."

She nudged the stones around her palm with her thumb.

"I didn't see any gold, but I think they're pretty. I'm going to take them home."

He finished sweeping and leaned the broom against a nearby boulder. "Can I see?"

She handed the stones over and watched him turn them around, holding them up to the light.

His brow drew down in a frown. "Where did you say you found these?"

"Up there." She pointed upstream. "About half a mile, I think. The flooding must have washed away the rock beneath them and made the bank collapse."

"Did you go past my claim markers?"

"No."

He handed the stones back to her. "Show me."

They left Brutus and R.B. dozing on a rock in the sunshine and she led him to the place where she'd found the stones. He stood with his hands on his hips, studying the collapsed section of the rock and dirt bank.

"So do you think they're quartz?"

"I can't be sure what they are. When I first bought the claim, I learned about the things I might find up here, but sometimes you need special equipment to tell for sure what something is."

She'd known him long enough to recognize when he was keeping something from her. "But what do you think they are?"

"I don't know."

"But you have an idea."

He blew out a long breath. "This is just a suspicion, mind. And it's likely wrong."

She took his arm and turned him to face her. "Will you stop dancing around the issue and tell me?"

He pressed his lips together. "They might, and they're probably not, but there's a very, very, *very* small chance they might *possibly* be diamonds."

It was a good ten seconds before she could gather her wits enough to say anything. "D-*diamonds*?"

"They're most likely not," he said quickly. "It's nothing to get your hopes up about."

"But... but... *diamonds*?!"

He laughed at the astonishment on her face. "I shouldn't have said anything."

"Oh no, you can't take it back now." She grasped his hand and tugged him over to the collapsed bank. "Let's see if we can find any more."

CHAPTER 24

The following day they traveled to Auburn in the buckboard, Brutus riding in the back. They were taking two of the probably-not diamonds to the assay office there, just to check.

Gabriel was almost sure they weren't diamonds. Yes, in his limited knowledge they looked like raw diamonds, but he refused to believe that they were. They couldn't be. He wasn't that lucky, except when it came to women. And then only when it came to Grace.

Of course, he'd heard the stories of places where you could pick diamonds up off the ground, but those were few and far between and had probably all been discovered by now anyway. And yes, he knew it was likely that bank had been there for hundreds, if not thousands of years and those stones could conceivably have been trapped there since they were formed. It was true that diamonds had been discovered relatively close by, but that didn't mean they would be on his claim.

The whole idea was ludicrous.

Wasn't it?

On reaching Auburn they went directly to the assay office, even though it had been a long drive. Neither of them wanted to wait for the answer about the stones.

Although they most definitely weren't diamonds. That would be impossible.

The armed guard inside the door nodded to Gabriel and tipped his hat to Grace.

"Good afternoon, Mr. Silversmith," the man behind the counter on the other side of the small front room said.

"Afternoon, Mr. Thompson," Gabriel replied, slightly taken aback. Even though he saw him every one or two months when he came in with the gold he'd collected, Mr. Thompson never remembered him. Maybe, after more than two years, he'd finally made an impression. "May I introduce my wife?"

Mr. Thompson nodded at Grace. "Ma'am. So how much have you got today?"

"I'm not here with gold this time," Gabriel said. "We'd like to see Mr. Cook, if he's available."

"I'll check if he can see you." He stood from the stool he sat on behind the counter. "What's it about?"

"We think we might have found diamonds," Grace said, before Gabriel could stop her.

Mr. Thompson's eyebrows reached for his receding hairline. "Diamonds?"

"They're probably not," Gabriel said quickly, before her excitement prompted her to offer more details. "I'm almost sure they're not, but we just thought we'd check. It's just a couple of tiny stones."

"Well, I'll see if Mr. Cook's free."

Once he'd left through a door into the rear of the building, Gabriel turned to Grace and lowered his voice. The guard had stepped outside, but he was still close to the door.

"It's probably best if you don't tell anyone about the diamonds. And don't mention them when other folks can overhear."

The excited smile melted from her face. "Oh, I didn't think. But surely he's not a danger? He works in the assay office. He must be around valuable jewels all the time."

"I'm sure you're right, but just in case."

Her smile returned. "So I suppose that means you do think there's a chance they're..." She looked around and then leaned in towards him, lowering her voice to a comically clandestine whisper. "...*real diamonds.*"

He snorted a laugh. "I didn't say that."

The door behind the counter opened and Mr. Thompson stepped back into the room. "Mr. Cook can see you now, if you'd like to follow me?"

Gabriel had never been anywhere but in the front room of the assay office, since all he ever brought in were small amounts of gold that Mr. Thompson dealt with himself. He'd somehow imagined a treasure trove of gold and jewels spilling from safes and drawers. All that lay beyond the door, however, was a thoroughly plain hallway.

"Just go on in," Mr. Thompson said, indicating the only open door.

They found themselves in a large, white-walled room containing several high, wooden tables sporting a range of scientific-looking paraphernalia. And not a hint of gold to be seen. The only person there was an older man with a neat, gray beard who sat at one of the tables, peering into a microscope. He looked up as they entered.

"So you think you've found diamonds," he said in a

bored voice that suggested he very much doubted it.

"Yes," Grace said immediately.

"Probably not," Gabriel added.

Mr. Cook held out his hand. "Let's see them then."

Gabriel took a pouch from inside his jacket, emptied the two stones into his palm, and handed them over.

He looked bored as he held them up. "Well I can tell you just from the size that these aren't..." He stopped. After a few seconds, he murmured a vague, "Hmm."

For the next twenty minutes he didn't say another word as he put the stones through a series of tests using the microscope, a series of hand lenses, and even removing a tiny chip from the corner of one, which made Gabriel wince.

After a while, he and Grace sat in two chairs by the wall to wait. He silently took Grace's hand.

Finally, Mr. Cook focused on them for the first time since they'd arrived. They both stood at once.

"I would never have believed it if I hadn't seen it with my own eyes, but what you have here are raw diamonds."

Grace gasped, her hand tightening almost painfully around Gabriel's.

He stared at Mr. Cook, speechless. Eventually, he started breathing again. "Could... could you repeat that?"

"Diamonds," he dutifully said again, "and good quality. Where did you get them?"

"Uh... I have a placer claim up in the mountains." They couldn't be real diamonds. It just wasn't possible.

"So you found them on your land?"

"Yes."

"There was a storm a couple of nights ago," Grace said.

"It washed away some rocks and a bank collapsed. That's where we found them."

Mr. Cook nodded. "Well, that would explain why stones this size haven't been discovered before now."

Gabriel swallowed. "How much are they worth?"

"As they are now, the smaller I'd put at around one and a half thousand dollars. The larger, two thousand. If you had them professionally cut, however, that value would rise considerably."

Gabriel was vaguely aware his mouth was hanging open. He glanced at Grace. She appeared no less shocked than he was.

"I can put you in touch with buyers, if you'd like," Mr. Cook said.

It took Gabriel a couple of tries to get his voice to work. "We have more of them."

One side of Mr. Cook's mouth curled up. "Then it looks like you are about to become very wealthy indeed."

~ ~ ~

It wasn't until after they had gone to a restaurant to eat and were on their way back to Green Hill Creek that either of them said anything about what had happened at the assay office.

"I still can't quite believe it," Grace said.

"Me neither."

He suspected he wouldn't believe it until he actually had the money. Things like this didn't happen to him. He couldn't shake the feeling that something would go wrong.

246

"Do you think Mr. Fowler's employers knew, and that's why they've been trying to buy the claim from you?"

That same idea had occurred to him. "I don't see how they could have known for sure, but I think they suspected. That's why they've been buying all the land around mine. They think there are diamonds in the area." The thought of how close he'd come to selling made him feel sick. "If it wasn't for you, I might have sold it. I would never have known those diamonds were there."

She nudged his arm with her shoulder. "So I suppose marrying me has been worth it after all."

He wrapped one arm around her and kissed her temple. "Marrying you is the best thing I've ever done, and diamonds have nothing to do with it."

They lapsed into silence, Grace resting against him with her head on his shoulder, just the way he liked it.

"I'm a bad person," she said after a while.

"Oh? How so?"

A smile spread across her face. "I can't stop thinking about how jealous Felicia is going to be when she finds out."

CHAPTER 25

Gabriel closed the gate to the pasture, slid both bolts into place, and headed for the house with Brutus trotting along beside him.

He looked around as he walked. He was more familiar with everything there than any place he'd lived since he'd left home, but now he viewed it through the eyes of a man who would soon have the means to change it. He had to admit, he wasn't at all sure what he would do. Improve the barns? Build new ones? Build onto the house? Have an entirely new house built? The possibilities made his head spin.

He'd never even dreamed of having as much money as the diamonds would bring. It was surprisingly daunting. But at least he wouldn't have to make those decisions alone.

Reaching the open door of the house, he leaned against the frame and watched Grace at the stove. She slid four pancakes from the frying pan onto a plate piled with several more keeping warm on the stove and replaced them with bacon, arranging the rashers around the pan.

Without even thinking about it, he was smiling.

When he'd asked a stranger on the far side of the country to marry him, not having any idea what she looked like or who she really was, he couldn't have dreamed how his life with her would be, how happy she would make him. Thirty-four years of his life lived in darkness, until he'd met her. Well, maybe darkness was a mite harsh, but that was what it felt like. She'd brought light and joy into his life. She'd taught him what true love was.

Brutus nudged his legs, pushing past him to follow the enticing smell of the bacon.

Gabriel pushed away from the doorframe and walked inside. "Breakfast smells good."

She glanced back at him. "I thought I'd do something extra nice. A celebratory breakfast."

He walked up behind her, slid his arms around her waist, and kissed the side of her neck. "I love all your cooking, but I do especially love your bacon and pancakes."

She turned around in his arms and treated him to her beautiful smile. "I..."

Brutus spun from the stove to face the door, a growl edging past his bared teeth.

"Silversmith! Get out here."

Gabriel stiffened at Fowler's voice.

He released Grace and marched for the door, grabbing his rifle on the way. "I swear, if that man doesn't leave us alone..."

He came to an abrupt halt on the porch.

Fowler stood in middle of the yard, a revolver in his hand. Three other men were with him, all of them armed, all of them holding their weapons.

He heard light footsteps behind him. Keeping his eyes on Fowler and his men, he said, "Grace, get back inside."

"Unless you want your husband shot, you'll stay out

249

here, Mrs. Silversmith," Fowler said.

All trace of his previous counterfeit cordiality had vanished. Gabriel was in no doubt that he would follow through with any threat.

"You leave her alone." He still held his rifle, the barrel pointed at the ground, for now.

Brutus, hackles raised, stalked to the edge of the porch and growled.

Fowler aimed his gun at the angry dog. "Put the rifle down, Silversmith, and lock the dog up or I'll shoot it."

Gabriel tightened his grip on the stock. You didn't let go of your weapon unless you had no other choice.

Grace wrapped her fingers around his arm. "Please. I don't want you to be hurt."

He glanced down at her frightened face and then back at Fowler and his men. There was no way he'd be able to shoot all of them before they fired back. He couldn't risk her being hurt.

Every battle-sharpened nerve screaming at him not to, he placed the rifle down on the porch then called Brutus. It took three sharp commands before his dog reluctantly obeyed and allowed Gabriel to get him back into the house.

Once the door was closed, Fowler beckoned to them with his revolver. "Now come on down here, both of you."

"Stay behind me," Gabriel murmured as he led the way down the stairs to the yard.

Grace's hand pushed into his. It was icy cold and trembling.

Fowler would pay for frightening his wife.

"What's this about?"

250

"I think you know what this is about. Heard you found yourself more than just gold up on your claim."

Gabriel kept his voice level. "Where'd you hear that?"

Fowler's mouth curled into a humorless smile. "Let's just say we have friends in the assay office."

"Thompson," he muttered. He'd known it was unusual when he remembered his name. Fowler must have been paying him to look out for Gabriel.

"So now we have a problem," Fowler went on. "See, those diamonds should belong to the people I work for. They would have, if you'd taken their very generous offer for that land at the start. You know, they only wanted to offer you a thousand, but I persuaded them to make it two. Didn't figure anyone would turn down two thousand dollars for a worn out claim. But you just had to be stubborn."

"Seeing as how things turned out," Gabriel said, "seems I was right to be stubborn."

"I don't think so, because now, as I said, we have a problem. My bosses want that claim. They've bought up a lot of land searching for those diamonds. Had a geologist or some such do surveys and he said the chances of there being diamonds here were high." He gave a sharp, hollow laugh. "Of course, it would turn out that they're on the only piece of land around that doesn't belong to them. Now they're not happy, and when they're not happy, I'm not happy."

"Can't say as I care if you're happy or not." He might have been able to reach the nearest of them and get his weapon before any of them could react, but the problem was Grace. How would he protect her?

"Well you should, because now I need that land from
251

you, and since you haven't exactly been cooperative up to this point we're going to have to do it the hard way." Fowler nodded to one of the men with him. "Chavez, take Mrs. Silversmith aside so Mr. Silversmith has some motivation to cooperate."

"Yes, Mr. Fowler." He stalked forward, his eyes fixed on Grace.

Gabriel moved between them, fists clenching. He had survived three years of war surrounded by blood and death, and had fought for his life and the life of his friends daily, but he had never experienced such a deep, primal terror as he felt with Grace in danger.

"You stay away from her."

"Get out of my way," Chavez growled, now only a few feet from them.

Lunging forward, Gabriel grabbed at his gun and thrust his arm upwards. Chavez tried to shove him away.

Their brief scuffle was brought to an abrupt halt by the sound of a gunshot. Barking erupted from the house.

"Silversmith," Fowler snapped, lowering his revolver, "if you don't stop now, the next bullet goes in your wife's head."

Gabriel sucked in a breath and looked between him and Chavez. Terrified as he was, he couldn't win, not like this.

Slowly, he released Chavez's arm and raised his hands. Chavez rammed his fist into his gut. A shock of pain shot through him, doubling him over, and all he could do was watch, helpless, as Chavez grasped Grace's wrist and pulled her to the side, pointing his revolver at her head.

"Gabriel!" Her frantic gaze found his and his heart broke

252

at the fear he saw there.

Please, God, he prayed desperately, *please protect her.*

Straightening, teeth gritted from the pain, he moved his gaze to Fowler. "What do you want?"

"What I've always wanted – that claim." He beckoned one of the other two men forward. "Davis has the papers ready for you to sign to transfer ownership to my employers. Give us that and any diamonds you've found and neither you nor your wife will get hurt. Refuse and she dies."

"No!" All eyes turned to Grace at her cry. Her eyes were fixed on Gabriel. "You can't. This is your dream."

He squeezed his eyes shut, desperately trying to think of another way. But there was none. All the diamonds in the world weren't worth one hair on her head.

Opening his eyes, he nodded once.

"Finally," Fowler said, motioning to Davis, "you see sense."

Davis walked forwards, lowering his rifle to reach inside his jacket. Gabriel briefly considered grabbing him when he got close enough, but he rejected the idea immediately. He had little doubt that Fowler would shoot even his own men rather than let anything get in his way.

Keeping as far back from Gabriel as he could, Davis pulled folded papers and a pen from his pocket and handed them over before stepping away and raising his rifle again.

Gabriel scanned the papers. It was a legal document to transfer the claim.

"Just sign at the bottom of both pages," Fowler said. "Then we'll leave you in peace."

Peace. After this, he wasn't sure he'd ever have peace

again. A sick feeling in the pit of his stomach, he signed the line at the foot of each page and handed them back to Davis who carried them to Fowler. He nodded to Chavez.

When he released Grace's wrist, she ran to Gabriel, throwing herself into his arms. He held her trembling body tight and glared at Fowler.

"You shouldn't have done it," she whispered, looking up at him. "That claim means everything to you."

Did she still not know how he felt about her?

He brushed a thumb across her cheek. "You're worth more to me than all the gold and all the diamonds in the world."

Her face lit up in awe. "Truly?"

Despite the circumstances, he managed a small smile. "Don't you know how much you mean to me?"

Fowler interrupted the moment. "Touching as this is, we should be going. Davis and Hinkle, take care of the dog and search the house for the diamonds. Chavez, kill them both."

Gabriel's heart hit his throat. "*What?*"

"You didn't think I'd leave you alive to tell the authorities, did you? When your bodies are discovered, they'll just assume bandits came, ransacked this place, and killed the two of you. It'll be a terrible tragedy." Fowler's smirk disappeared as he addressed Chavez. "Do it."

"With pleasure," he replied, raising his pistol.

A window shattered and a snarling blur hurtled off the porch, crashing into Chavez and throwing him to the ground. His gun spun away across the dirt.

Gabriel launched himself at Davis, grabbing for the barrel of his rifle. It fired as he shoved it into the air, the sound slamming into his skull. Ignoring his ringing ears, he rammed his boot into Davis' gut and wrenched the rifle from his grasp.

There was a flurry of movement from the direction of the pasture and Hinkle yelped, pitching forward onto his face. Goat jumped onto his back and bleated.

Too late, Gabriel saw Fowler swing his revolver in his direction.

Another shot ripped through the air.

Fowler's eyes widened and he looked down at an expanding spot of red on his chest.

For a moment, everything was still.

And then he collapsed.

Grace held Chavez's pistol, the muzzle still aimed at where Fowler had stood.

Davis staggered backwards and thrust his hands into the air above him. "Don't shoot!"

"On your face on the ground!" Gabriel barked.

He obeyed immediately.

"Grace, are you all right?"

Turning her eyes slowly to Gabriel, she said in a small voice, "I shot him." She still hadn't lowered the gun.

"Yes, you did."

"Is he dead?"

He glanced at Fowler's still form. "I don't know."

She licked her lips and swallowed. "I don't want him to be dead, but he was going to shoot you."

"You did the right thing. You saved my life." He wanted to take her into his arms and never let go, but he couldn't do anything until Davis and Hinkle were incapacitated. "Do you think you could get some rope from the barn?"

She moved her eyes from Fowler, finally lowering the pistol. "I... yes. Rope."

He'd seen enough soldiers experience their first battle to know she was in shock. But, unlike many of them, she hadn't frozen. She'd responded to the danger, she'd taken action, and she'd saved him. He couldn't have been more proud.

She started in the direction of the barn. After a couple of steps she stopped, changed direction, and walked slowly towards Fowler. The papers transferring ownership of Gabriel's claim lay on the ground by his hand, fluttering in the slight breeze. She bent to pick them up, ripped them into pieces, and pushed them into her pocket. Then she picked up Fowler's gun and resumed walking to the barn. Goat jumped down from Hinkle's back and trotted after her.

When she returned with the rope, he bound Davis and Hinkle and went to check on Fowler. To his relief, he was breathing. He didn't want Grace to have to live with the knowledge that she'd killed a man. He knew what that was like and it was the last thing he wanted for her. Of course, Fowler might still die, but he hoped she would never find out about it.

With the immediate danger over, he drew her into his arms and held her tight against him, silently thanking God. "Are you all right?" he whispered into her hair.

"I will be."

"We'll take them into town to the marshal. Can you get Fred and Jed ready while I deal with them?"

She drew in a deep breath, looked up at him, and nodded. "I can do that."

The color was returning to her face. She would be fine. His wife was strong.

"Can someone get this dog off me? I can't breathe."

They looked at Chavez where he lay pinned on his back on the ground, Brutus sprawled across him. The window Brutus had crashed through lay in a wreckage of glass and wood on the porch. As they watched, R.B. walked up to them, sniffed at Chavez, and climbed up his shoulder. Chavez's frantic protestations were swallowed in a mouthful of fur as the kitten sat on his face and sank his tiny, razor-sharp claws into his forehead.

Grace snorted delicately, raising smiling eyes to Gabriel, and he grinned back.

They left the task of freeing Chavez until last.

CHAPTER 26

When they finally arrived back home, it was past midday.

Chavez, Davis and Hinkle were in jail. Fowler was still with Doctor Wilson, but would be moved into a jail cell when he was done being treated. Deputy Filbert was with him to keep him in line.

The bullet had gone straight through his torso, just missing a lung. Fowler wasn't out of danger yet, but an inch one way or the other and he would have been dead. When Doctor Wilson told them, Grace had burst into tears.

"I think I might need to build a higher fence," Gabriel remarked as he brought the buckboard to a halt in the yard. "Now that Goat knows she can jump that one, she'll probably try it again."

"She should get extra supper today though," Grace said.

He smiled. "Yeah."

She climbed down from the buckboard without waiting for him to help her and started towards the house. All she wanted to do was get back into her home and sit down. The events of the morning had left her exhausted.

Seeing the red patch where Fowler had lain after she shot him, she came to a halt.

She didn't regret what she'd done. If she could have

gone back and done it all over again, she would still have grabbed the gun from the ground when she saw Fowler aim at Gabriel, still brought it up just as he'd taught her, squeezing the trigger as her arm rose. Nothing could make her sorry for saving her husband. But she hoped she would never have to do anything like it again.

Gabriel walked up beside her and touched her arm. "You all right?"

With a deep sigh she turned and buried her face in his chest, sliding her arms around his waist. He immediately wrapped his arms around her, holding her close.

"Why do I feel this way?" she said into his shirt. "He was going to kill both of us and I know I did what I had to, and yet I still feel so guilty. Why?"

His hand rubbed gentle circles on her back. "I had a lot of guilt like that after the war. I know I didn't choose to fight, but it still ate at me. Maybe that's what separates us from people like Fowler. Sometimes we're forced to do things we don't want to, but it affects us. If it didn't, we'd be as bad as they are."

She considered his words. "You're right." Raising her head, she cupped his face in both hands and gazed into his beautiful brown eyes. "You're a good man, Gabriel. I'm so blessed to be your wife."

Eyes misting over, he lowered his head to her shoulder and pressed his face into her neck. They stood that way for a while, holding each other tight, silently gaining strength just from being together.

Until a large, furry head pushed between them.

Grace laughed and placed her hand on Brutus' head.

259

"I'm proud of you too, Brutus. You saved both of us. How about some sausages for lunch?"

As if knowing exactly what she was saying, he wagged his tail. It was probably the word sausages.

She was about to step from Gabriel's embrace when a look of sadness passed across his face.

She touched one hand to his jaw. "What's wrong?"

His chest rose and fell in a sigh and he gazed across the valley. "When we get the money from the diamonds, will you want to leave here? I know you don't like living so far from town and being so isolated."

She glanced around her. Gabriel's house had seemed so small to her at the beginning. Now, though, she thought of it as her home, and she loved it. It was cozy and warm and filled with laughter and love. She'd found real happiness in that tiny one-roomed house and, even though she'd only been there a short time, she couldn't imagine living anywhere else.

"Do you want to leave?"

He moved his gaze back to her. "No, but I will, for you."

He was telling the truth, she knew. All her adult life, all she'd wanted was a man who truly cared for her. Gabriel was the answer to all her prayers.

"Then it's a good thing I don't want to leave either."

His eyes flicked between hers. "You really mean that?"

"With all my heart."

A smile blossoming on his lips, he dipped his face to hers and murmured, "I love you."

The kiss lasted a good five seconds before Brutus pushed further between them with a whine.

She should have known better than to mention sausages.

CHAPTER 27

Four years later.

Grace gazed out over the valley, rocking gently back and forth on the swinging bench on the porch.

A cool breeze ruffled her hair and she looked down at the baby in her lap, tucking the blanket more securely around her. Martha pressed her pink lips together and stretched her legs, but her eyes remained firmly closed.

On the seat beside her, R.B. yawned, stretched his huge body to its full length, then curled up again, flicking one ear and closing his eyes. Brutus snored at her feet.

She loved lazy afternoons relaxing on the bench Gabriel had built for her during her first pregnancy. She always had a book with her, but often she would simply sit and enjoy her view. Even though she knew it so well, she noticed new things almost every day.

It had been the most important consideration when the new house was built, to have a porch from which she could see the valley. It was her favorite spot, just as the porch on the old house had been. They'd even had the new house built where it didn't block the view from their old, one-roomed home, just so she could still sit there when she wanted to.

Although when their children grew, they planned to turn it into a play house.

She watched the buckboard approach, waving as Gabriel drove past the front lawn and around to the barns. She smiled as she listened to the voices as he unhitched the buckboard, followed by bleating and giggles as he put Fred and Jed into the pasture while avoiding letting Goat out.

A minute later, he plodded around the corner of the house, legs apart, picking each foot up slowly as if it was unusually heavy. Of course, that could have been due to the fact that he had a small boy seated on each boot, wrapped around his calves.

"Grace, I have some disturbing news."

She carefully didn't smile. "You do?"

He nodded gravely. "I do. I seem to have lost the boys."

"That certainly is disturbing news. Where have you looked?"

"Everywhere." He held one hand up to shield his eyes and peered across the yard. "I can't think where they could be."

Charlie giggled. Joe shushed him.

"Have you by any chance checked your feet?"

He looked down and gasped in a comically shocked breath. "There you are!"

The twins erupted into laughter and squeals as he leaned down to lift one in each arm, spun them around, and kissed each of them soundly on the forehead.

When he put them down they ran to the porch as fast as their short legs would carry them and clambered up the steps. Gabriel followed more sedately.

Grace reached out a free arm to hug Joe when he ran up to her. "Did you have fun in town?"

Charlie looked up at her from where he had his arms wrapped around Brutus' neck. "Pa bought us a licorice stick each."

"Did he? Well that was kind of him." And not at all a surprise given his inability to refuse his sons anything. She looked up at him and he shrugged and smiled.

"We saw Emily," Joe said, taking Martha's tiny hand when she stretched it out.

Charlie moved on to R.B. who raised his head from the bench and patiently endured his gentle hug.

"That's nice," Grace replied, kissing the top of Charlie's head when he finally made it to her.

Joe always wanted his mother, but for Charlie, Brutus and R.B. took precedence.

Having completed his round of hugs, Charlie patted his leg. "Come on, Brutus. Come and play."

Brutus hauled himself to his feet and followed the two boys back down to the lawn, tongue hanging out and tail wagging.

Gabriel walked up to the bench, leaned down to kiss Grace, and stroked a hand over R.B.'s head. "I'd like to sit next to my wife, please."

R.B. opened one eye, stared at him for a second, then closed it again.

Gabriel heaved a sigh. "Fine."

Wrapping his hands around the cat's middle, he hauled him up from the bench, sat, and put him down beside him. R.B. cast him a reproving look and jumped down to the porch where he sauntered to the edge of the steps and sat down to lick a paw.

On the lawn, Brutus woofed and Charlie and Joe giggled as he bounded after them.

"How were the boys in town?" Grace said.

"Perfectly behaved, as always. Well, Joe was." He pulled an envelope from his pocket and handed it to her, exchanging it for their daughter. "Adam gave me that for you. We met Jo and Emily in the general store. She invited us for lunch on Sunday after church." He kissed Martha's forehead and settled her on his lap, facing him. "How's my little girl? Have you said your first word yet? Can you say 'Pa'?"

Grace tore open the top of the envelope and pulled out the letter inside. "Fairly sure three weeks is a little young to be talking."

"My little girl is smart, just like her mama." He rubbed the tip of his nose across Martha's and she opened her eyes and blinked up at him. He smiled. "And beautiful, just like her mama."

From the moment she was born, he'd been smitten with his daughter, just like he was with their twin boys. Grace couldn't have wished for a better father for her children.

"Is it from your father?" he said.

"Mm hmm." She scanned the two page missive, bursting into laughter when she reached the first sentence on page two. "Listen to this. 'I've had to put my foot down on Felicia's plans for the nursery. She wanted to cover the cradle in gold leaf.' Maybe he's finally coming to his senses." Her heart missed a beat as she continued to read. "He says he wants to come and visit once the baby is born and old enough to

265

travel. He wants to meet you and his grandchildren, and he wants me to meet my new brother or sister."

She pressed her lips together, reading the lines again. She hadn't seen her father in four years, since she'd left to marry Gabriel. They corresponded regularly, but neither had suggested a visit. Even though their letters were friendly, she hadn't thought he wanted to see her again.

A tear rolled down her cheek as she read the final sentences in her father's hand.

I do miss you very much, Grace. I know I haven't been the best of fathers, but you're my daughter and a day doesn't go by when I don't regret what happened to drive you away. Felicia falling pregnant has reminded me what a deep responsibility being a father is, and after your mother died I failed in that responsibility. I know I can't make up for that, but if you are agreeable, I'd like to try to be a better father, and grandfather, from now on.

Your mother would be so very happy that you've named your first daughter after her.

You'll always be my little girl.

All my love,

Daddy.

Gabriel wrapped his arm around her and kissed her temple. "You okay?"

"Yes." She wiped at her eyes and rested her head against his shoulder. "You wouldn't care if it took Martha a long time to find the right husband for her, would you?"

"Course not. I'm not planning on letting any man court her until she's thirty-five anyway."

She pressed her face against his chest, laughing. "You're the world's best father. And you're going to be the world's most nightmarish father-in-law."

He grinned. "You bet I am."

Out on the lawn, Brutus flopped down into the grass. Tired out from their trip into town, Charlie and Joe nestled in beside him, resting their heads on his flank. All three would be asleep in minutes, like always.

Gabriel's smile faded. "I know what your father did hurt you, but I can't say I regret that he did it. If he hadn't, I wouldn't have gotten myself the most wonderful wife a man could wish for."

Even after four years of marriage, he could still make her heart flutter. She reached up to kiss him softly. "And I wouldn't have gotten myself the most wonderful husband a woman could wish for. With not a hairy ear in sight."

He chuckled softly. "Will you leave me if I ever grow hair in my ears?"

She kissed him again and settled back against his chest. "I will adore you until the day I die."

"Even my hairy ears?"

Snuggling against him, she closed her eyes and smiled in perfect contentment.

"Even your hairy ears."

THE END

DEAR READER

Thank you for reading More Than Gold and I hope you've enjoyed Gabriel and Grace's story. Who would have guessed, after his less than gentlemanly behavior in The Truth About Love, that Gabriel would turn out to be such a sweetheart? I'll be honest, he surprised even me! I think he always had it in him to be a good man, he just needed the right woman to motivate him.

Next in the series is *The Judge's Daughter*. George Parsons never counted on falling in love again, until Millicent came along. But he'll have to travel to New York and overcome snobbery, prejudice and danger to win her heart.

If you have a moment, I would love for you to leave a review for More Than Gold to help other readers to find it.

If you haven't already, you can subscribe to my newsletter on my website and I'll send you an ebook of the prequel novella *The Blacksmith's Heart* for free. And if you'd like to get in touch with me, visit my website or Facebook page, or email me at nerys@nerysleigh.com. I love to hear from readers!

nerysleigh.com
facebook.com/nerysleigh

31763287R00166

Made in the USA
San Bernardino, CA
07 April 2019